ALSO BY

SÉLIM NASSIB

I Loved You for Your Voice

THE PALESTINIAN
LOVER

Sélim Nassib

THE PALESTINIAN LOVER

*Translated from the French
by Alison Anderson*

Europa
editions

Europa Editions
116 East 16th Street
New York, N.Y. 10003
www.europaeditions.com
info@europaeditions.com

Translation by Alison Anderson
Original title: *Un amant en Palestine*
Translation copyright © 2007 by Europa Editions

This work has been published thanks to support from
the French Ministry of Culture – Centre National du Livre
Ouvrage publié avec le concours du Ministère
Français chargé de la Culture – Centre National du Livre

Library of Congress Cataloging in Publication Data is available
ISBN-13: 978-1-933372-23-5
ISBN-10: 1-933372-23-0

Nassib, Sélim
The Palestinian Lover

Book design by Emanuele Ragnisco
www.mekkanografici.com

Printed in Italy
Arti Grafiche La Moderna – Rome

CONTENTS

I wrote in free association with her,
the scaffolding came down,
the flesh-and-blood story appeared behind
the words which had become transparent.
And the all-devouring love
which binds us, her and me,
has been mysteriously embodied
in this book, laid bare
by her grace. To Yo Z.

In the latter years of the 1920s, Lebanon was under French mandate, Palestine under British mandate, borders were still freshly drawn and they were virtually the same country.

In those years, the Jews who watched as the shores of Palestine approached had the feeling that they were drawing closer to the reality of their life. They recognized the hills, the original names. They saw themselves emerging from the shadow to take shape at last, to have a body at last. The proof of their feeling prevented them from even putting a face to the nameless figures who were present on their land. They were coming home after such a long absence.

The Arabs looked upon them as dangerous cranks who had thrust themselves upon their landscape. It was the fault of the British. Even a child would understand that it was pure madness to want to create one country in place of another. The streets, the people, the earth, history, the region: everything made it impossible. For centuries an assortment of people intoxicated with Jerusalem had wound up in Palestine, their heads filled with utopias. But these ones were stubborn. They were digging in and moving forward as if their stubbornness could be harder than stone, their dream stronger than reality. It was ridiculous.

And yet, year after year, the signs have been inexplicably reversed, the Jewish state has become a reality, and it is the Palestinian people who have become ghosts. They have changed places, body for body.

*

At the end of the 1920s, Albert Pharaon was living in Lebanon. He belonged to a wealthy Palestinian family, dabbled as a banker, but felt rather out of place in Beirut. He was bored by society life; horses were his sole passion. He often went back to Haifa, his birthplace, three hours by road, until finally he settled there again, abandoning his wife and children. The scandalous news ignited and spread: Albert had a Jewish mistress in Palestine, her name was Golda Meir.

I've always been familiar with this story: Albert Pharaon was the grandfather of my friend Fouad. It seemed utterly unbelievable to me. How could the pasionaria of Zionism—its very incarnation, one might say—find herself in the arms of a Palestinian lover?

One of Albert's nieces is still living, in Cairo. She has always felt as though she were in exile there. When she was a very young woman her family had forced her to marry a rich Egyptian. Albert went to see her whenever he was in Cairo, and she was as fond of horses as he was. He told her about Golda, there was no one else he could talk to. The rest of the family preferred not to know. One of their own sleeping with the enemy . . . there was something inconceivable about it, indecent, almost obscene.

In Tel Aviv there is not the slightest trace. Golda Meir's children, her biographer, are dumbfounded. Golda loved men, but her lovers were Jewish, as was her world; she knew no other men. Except, perhaps, for one night, King Abdullah of Transjordan. It seems like some fantasy, a fiction dreamt up by the Pharaon family.

An impossible story? *Almost* impossible, obliged to unfold in the tiny space of this *almost*, where things that should not happen do happen, the narrow patch of earth where forbidden flowers grow, instinctive impulses, life itself.

1

Kibbutz · 1923

Regina has put on the new white dress she brought with her just in case. She turns from side to side in the damp, drab room, baring her legs. Blond, tanned, and curvaceous, she is almost beautiful, with her mischievous eyes and that funny smile which causes the corners of her mouth to tremble. This is the first sunny April day after a week of torrential rain. Sabbath eve, and the weather is too fine to go back to Jerusalem. Nazareth is a foreign place to her, she knows no one there. Now she is lost with her luggage on a street where one meets only Arabs—they pass her by without seeming to notice her. She sits down on her suitcase to wait. That is what she does when she doesn't know what else to do. The damp earth is making her drowsy, she is nodding off. A curious peasant—there is always one about—climbs down from his cart and comes up to her:

"Kibbutz?"

He seems to want to help her. She gets up.

After one last bend in the road, the forms of Mount Thabor appear, round and feminine, eroded by the centuries. Above the horizon, the setting sun illuminates the clouds from within, like mountains projected onto the sky, shot through with colors. The kibbutz seems tiny beneath such a weight, as if flattened between sky and earth. For Regina, the vision is almost supernatural. In Milwaukee she knew nothing but the teeming life of the Walnut Street Jewish neighborhood where she grew up. She would still be there if at the age of eight Golda had not arrived in her town, in her class, in her street. She had so loved that little Russian girl that she was ready to follow her to the ends of the earth.

The stench of the swamp always surprises Regina. Later, it will become part of the air she breathes. The old mule edges slowly along the pebbly road, but makes headway. Close up, the kibbutz seems to huddle upon itself, surrounded by an ugly cement wall punctured here and there with arrow slits. The cart stops outside. Above the wooden gate an armed man stands watch. In the contre-jour his body and rifle form a single silhouette.

Bent over his reins the Arab peasant waits in another world. The valley, which the Jews call the Wide Spaces of God, is for him simply the dead swamp. The man walking toward them with a nonchalant gait seems to have forgotten he is carrying a rifle. His khaki shirt hangs loose over his oversized pants. He walks around the cart. His green eyes draw a line of color in his dark brown face. He speaks neither English nor Yiddish nor Hebrew nor Arabic, but a mixture that grows all the more unintelligible with the increasing confusion of his feelings as he beholds the young blond woman in a white dress. She jumps down. He pulls out his passport and shows it to her: he is Iranian, an Iranian Jew. He says, in English, *first day*, and she understands that it is his first day at the kibbutz.

The peasant maneuvers his cart to turn around. His coat is the color of the wood on the cart. He resembles the mountains and the earth around him. Regina runs behind him and holds out a banknote. He refuses to be paid.

She is through the gate; she is at home. The kibbutz is spread over a square of roughly a hundred meters in length. There is no one there. In the middle is a one-story brick building flanked by a tall water tank. With her suitcase in her hand the young woman walks down the lane which the rain has transformed into a muddy path. In the sunlight the huts look freshly built, and leaves have appeared on the trees. The vegetable garden has doubled in surface. Regina leans over and gently strokes the shoots; their tender green contrasts sharply with the dark earth. A new warehouse has been built. Through the window she glimpses men and woman wearing white kerchiefs, working beneath a glaring light around a sort of incubator.

Regina puts down her luggage. The dormitories are nothing more than a double row of wooden bunks spread with blankets in faded colors. Privacy is forbidden here. The architecture of the kibbutz makes that much clear, certainly these dormitories. Nothing is sacrificed to comfort or esthetics, everything to communal life. Regina adores this rectitude, but only for a few days. Two years ago, when Golda and Morris wanted to enter into this human bubble, their request was initially turned down because they were married.

Two or three sentries, their rifles over their shoulders, are peacefully standing guard around the field where scattered human forms huddle close to the earth. Regina cannot get used to the way they are dressed. Men and women alike are clothed in a rough fabric, held closed by a simple rope around the waist, in which holes have been made for the head and the arms. Their faces, hands, and any other exposed parts of their skin have been covered over with grease in order to trick what the Arabs call the *barghash*, a cloud of mosquitoes, flies and sand midges which infest one's eyes, ears and nostrils. The goal, day after day beneath a pitiless sun, is to dry out the swamp so they can plant seeds and saplings.

The young woman finds Morris at the bottom of a ditch. Armed with a stake, he is trying to break through the rocky surface to reach the earth beneath. Sweat has formed an aureole in his back. She calls to him softly.

"Morris!"

Golda's husband raises his head. He is unrecognizable. In his sunken grease-covered face his eyes behind their circular metal frames have become very large. They radiate with fever. His smile is all the more magnificent. He tosses his stake to one side, stands straight, holding his lower back, and climbs painfully out of his hole. He opens his arms to her:

"I'm too dirty to hold you against me."

"I don't care!" she cries, rushing toward him.

He removes his dust-smeared glasses, and this leaves him with two clear circles around his eyes. He is trembling slightly, but continues to smile. She looks at his hands. They are covered with blisters, many of which have already burst, and blood oozes from his wounds. Morris is a cellist.

"Are you all right?" she murmurs.

He stares at her, delighted and absent.

"Golda isn't here. She'll only get back tonight."

"Morris, are you all right?"

"It's hard, but it's okay. Look!"

She turns around. The sunset has lit a fire. Red and black run together, veiling the landscape in a blood-hued, end-of-the-world light. Morris remains silent.

"It's even more poignant when the work is so absurd . . . and so desperate," he murmurs finally, in a quiet voice.

"Desperate?"

"Yes. No one can undertake such a task and hope for the slightest profit. We're working for something else, no doubt."

"What?"

"I don't know . . . Jews were forbidden to work the land for so many centuries that here they take to it like lunatics. It's almost mystical, even if we're not believers."

"This is you speaking in this way?"

"Yes, me. This animal impulse that inhabits the kibbutzniks is more moving to me than I can say. But I don't feel it myself, and that's something I bitterly regret, because it's the only way to survive in this hellish place."

On the ramparts, there is the sound of a bell. The volunteer slave laborers back slowly out of their holes, one after the other, stumbling in the mud, their tools on their shoulders. Regina moves forward as if keeping step with a march of the living dead. A Hebrew chant rises on the air, a woman's voice, unusual, somewhat broken but strong, and the shapeless earth-colored figures take up the refrain. Regina shivers. She is one of the last in the procession. Morris, walking next to her, is so exhausted that he can barely put one foot in front of the other. With his eyes half-closed he is like a drunk who has passed out yet is still standing.

Men and women enter the courtyard and head straight for the showers. They toss off their rags and throw them in a pile by the entrance. Regina moves aside. Morris stops at the door. To shower naked with the others is something he still cannot do.

In the hut that serves as a refectory, Regina makes her way through the kibbutzniks surrounding her friend. Golda is radiant. The mass of hair tied back against the nape of her neck enhances her face, grown much more assured. Her beauty is sharper. Her body is stronger, hardened through trial. She moves well among all these men. All her determination is focused in her tight lips, fine as a blade. Regina can see in her eyes the same flame, the same terrible desire to devour the world—but this time it would seem the feast has begun. Golda is like a young olive tree growing rough and strong in an arid soil. When she notices her friend approaching, her face lights up, her gray-blue eyes crease with delight. The two women fall into each other's arms, look at one another and embrace again.

"I'm so happy you're here!" says Golda, intertwining her fingers with Regina's. "Stay with me."

She turns to the others.

"If you only knew how much I missed you! I don't know how to thank you for choosing me as your delegate. When we're working here in our corner, night and day, without ever looking up, we can sometimes begin to feel isolated. I'm back from Degania now with this message: we are not alone! A great movement is taking shape in Eretz Israel! Not only in the kibbutzim but also in the towns, the factories, the trade unions, the entire *yishuv*! Even in my dreams I could never have imagined that my eyes would see what they have seen in the last three days. We are alive! And we have the strength, the courage, and the faith to go all the way!"

Paralyzed with fatigue, the kibbutzniks take her in their arms. They are twenty years old, they live together. They obey their self-imposed Draconian egalitarian rules with an adolescent exaltation. It scarcely matters that they are thin and famished. Everything that might happen to them is happening for the first time. Their backbones have grown straighter, they have set themselves free from the ghettos of central Europe and from their parents. Morris is sitting at the corner of the table, smiling with admiration from afar, visibly too tired to remain on his feet. Golda joins him and encircles his head with her arms. He seems happy. They all seem happy, it's not really clear what has made them happy, they don't even question it. Their eyes are alert, altogether too human, a gaze that is hard to sustain. They spend their time singing. Their bodies are a chaos of desire and Hasidic dance.[1] They've left their religion behind, but the trance endures. It is Sabbath night.

Morris lifts his fork and lets it fall again as if it were too heavy for him:

"I'm not hungry. I think I'll go to bed now," he says to his wife.

"I'm coming with you."

He gestures no with his hand and rises painfully to his feet. He is trembling all over. Golda goes with him. Regina watches

---

[1] As a reaction to a serious religious crisis, Hasidism was founded in the 18th century in central Europe by a man who would be known as Baal Shem (or Baal Shem Tov). Members of the sect practiced a popular faith which was accessible to the masses, founded on joy and dance, unlike the gravity and hermetic practice of the Jewish religion. Hasidism was opposed to Zionism.

as he leaves, unsteady on his legs, stubbornly refusing his wife's support. At the door she lets him go, and comes back to have dinner.

It is three in the morning. On the ramparts, Golda leads her friend by the hand and points her in the direction of the farthest outlook post. In Milwaukee, Regina occasionally went to sleep over at Golda's, and they would spend their nights talking. Golda was haunted by the anti-Semitism she had known in Russia, and told her the same terrible stories over and over. Regina would put her arms around her and try to reassure her, but Golda invariably wore a stubborn air while tears of rage welled in her eyes. She would say no more, her expression remained fierce and absent, as if she could not hear, as if she had stayed there in Kiev where she was born. For her, the past was not dead, she was not ready to toss it out the window the way earlier immigrants advised the newcomers to do. America was not the end of the road. For as long as the safety and the destiny of the Jews did not depend on them alone, she would say, they could not see themselves as having *arrived*. This unshakable conviction had brought her to Palestine. And now, seeing her so luminous on the ramparts of the kibbutz, so poised and confident, Regina can understand how her friend has changed: she has arrived. At last she has been able to exhale the sigh of relief that was trapped in her chest for so many years. And this thing which has always prevented her from living—her inner rage, the sense of something missing, the insecurity—has now, it would seem, finally released its hold.

"When I went up to the podium and began to speak in Yiddish," said Golda, "the entire audience began to shout, 'Speak in Hebrew!' And when I tried to explain that in the kibbutz working in the kitchen was no more dishonorable than working in the fields, the women jumped to their feet, shouting, raising their fists, as if feeding the animals were somehow more noble than feeding people! I was the voice of a return to domestic oppression, and they were going to eat me alive. Among the delegates there were anarchists, socialist-Zionists, revisionists, militarists, mystics, utopists . . . I was able to show all of these people that our kibbutz was among the leaders in terms of egalitarianism, division of labor and an absence of discrimination between men and women. And the same thing for self-sufficiency, in other words setting a limit on resorting to Arab laborers."

Two figures, enlaced, are sitting deep within a niche in the rampart walk. The man sits up abruptly, revealing the young woman he was kissing. Narrowing her gaze, Regina recognizes the Iranian who had met her at the gate. The girl could hardly be older than eighteen, almost Nordic in her features, a pretty girl. Aviva, a new arrival. As if the couple were transparent, Golda continues:

"The Jews who are getting off the ships in Tel Aviv these days are immune to any sort of pioneering ideal. They just want to be left alone, as they are. The ones with money want to improve their production costs by hiring Arab laborers. If everyone goes on only looking out for themselves, before long the *yishuv* will turn into a bunch of refugees and hucksters. That's why the kibbutz is so extremely important. We embody the ideal. We are making the land fruitful, our land, and we are making it our own again. We are doing it in the service of a national community in the midst of a full renaissance, but we're also doing it for ourselves, for a good, righteous life, just there on the horizon."

Regina, leaning against the wall, is watching the young Iranian sitting cross-legged not far from her. He seems to be drifting in this strange light, his spirit free. His eyes are no more than two narrow slits looking back at her, Regina, unflinchingly. She looks away suddenly. Golda goes on talking, but Regina is no longer listening. Beyond the wall, everything is silent. It feels as if an invisible wave is flowing over her body, a wave from the landscape. When she raises her eyes, she sees Aviva coming up to her:

"And you," asks the young girl, staring at her, "where do you live?"

"In Jerusalem. I work at the Zionist office. That's why I speak Hebrew better than Golda does."

"What's that, the Zionist office?"

"A place everyone passes through sooner or later. Fanatics and businessmen alike, adventurers, believers, crooks, madmen . . . "

Aviva nods and falls silent. The three women remain motionless, one standing and the other two sitting. Regina succumbs to the pleasure of that strange feeling that came over her. Zev, the Ukrainian giant on guard, comes up to them:

"It's a quiet night. The villages are all dark, they must be sleeping with their fists closed."

He sits down. Golda reaches for a cigarette, he takes one from her and passes the packet on to the others. The moon marks a hole in the milky sky, casting a liquid light as far as the horizon. They smoke and observe the night.

"Have you ever listened to the *shofar*[2] in the final hours of Yom Kippur?" asks the Ukrainian giant. "If you listen carefully, you can hear two distinct sounds: a first long and melodious one which means 'There is order, the sun rises and sets, the spirit of God reigns over the earth as in the heavens.' And a second one, stifled, halting, tragic, which says, 'This is a world where the father kills his own child, and all is mere chaos and madness!' That second sound is Sarah's cry. When she understands that Abraham nearly sacrificed their son upon God's command, without saying a word to her, she let out a terrible cry and fell down dead. So the sacrifice of Isaac really was a

[2] Ram's horn used by rabbis for ritual music during certain holidays.

sacrifice, but it was Sarah who was the victim. That happened in Hebron, a few miles from here."

"No society can survive if it refuses to sacrifice its children," says Golda, very softly.

They are alone again. They head back in the dark.

"What are you going to do about Morris?" asks Regina.

"It's terrible for him."

"So I see."

"The slightest detail, and he is beside himself. We're not allowed to drink a cup of tea just the two of us in our room. That drives him mad. The toilets are on the far side of the yard, it's unbearable when it's cold, and at night, and above all when he's got a fever . . . And besides, those four holes stink! He simply can't take it."

"Is he blaming you in any way?"

"Morris never blames me for anything."

"He's not jealous?"

"Of course he's jealous, but he never says a thing. Well, there is one thing: he refuses with all his soul the idea of children being raised collectively. I've always wanted children, and so has he. But he doesn't want to watch them grow up in some nursery where he's only allowed to visit at certain times, and where you never really know whose child is who. He's followed me to Palestine, but if I want children, I'll have to follow him out of the kibbutz."

"Could you do that?"

"I don't know. This is as far as we've come . . . I'm stalling for time. He loves me and I love him, that much is clear. But I can't just give up this life which makes me happy and which is my life!"

"You know something? I think he's a wonderful person, Morris. The only thing here that's helping him survive is his phonograph. He didn't ask for this, to set off for Palestine, to scratch at some ungrateful clump of earth in the middle of a community of people who live with weapons in their hands. But he's doing exactly that, all the same, and doing all of it, for the love of a woman."

"That's true. His mother wrote to him. She offered to pay for his ticket back to America, on the condition that he go back without me."

"Nice as ever, his mother. But how is he supposed to decide? It's pathetic, watching him listen to his records over and over, ad nauseum."

"If we give up now, it will prove that the kibbutz was right: this kind of life is not possible for couples. And I just can't accept such a conclusion."

Regina was well-acquainted with her friend's hard and obstinate tone, and she was scarcely surprised. But behind Golda's assertive statement she sensed something other than her habitual stubbornness: a pleasure, a sort of delight that was totally unfamiliar to her.

"I get the feeling something happened to you in Degania."

"Yes, it's true," said Golda, bluntly. "Something I shall never forget. They were all there, the two Bens, Ben Gurion and Ben Zvi, and Katznelson, and Levi Eshkol and David Remez. Can you imagine? Just six or seven men, and the entire future of Eretz Israel rests on their shoulders."

"What are they like, close up?"

"Ben Gurion is really so exceptional that you hardly dare look at him. But they're all handsome, and passionate, and real balls of energy. You can't imagine what it's like, running into them all day long, calling them by their first name."

"Did they notice you?"

"Last night, at dinner, David Remez came and sat next to me."

"Did you sleep together?"

"We spent the night talking. I've never been that close to such a powerful man."

"And did he like you?"

"I think so . . . But they don't accept women in their midst
all that easily. They were interested in me because I speak English and most of their dealings are with the Anglo-Saxon
world."

"And?"

"And nothing. They said they might need me someday. They
know where to find me. In reality, it's over. Everyone went
their own way, and I came back here."

"Aren't you happy?"

"I'm delighted. This life is so fulfilling, I'm incredibly lucky,
I couldn't dream of anything better."

Regina gets undressed in the dormitory to the sound of sleep-
ers breathing heavily. Every time she comes to Merhavia, the
same ambivalent feelings overwhelm her: there is the pleasure of
being at the kibbutz, and the pleasure of getting ready to leave
again. She always leaves with a feeling of having been scrubbed
clean, ready to start from scratch. But it's too much; even Golda
is too much. I do like her, thinks Regina, but I'm not sure I
would like to be around so much intensity all the time.

Golda calls to her from the far end of the dormitory: "Regina, quick!"

In what passes for a separate bedroom, filled with the furniture Morris has made himself, Regina finds Golda in tears,
squeezing her husband's hands. Morris is lying helpless in his
bed, covered in an icy sweat, trembling from head to foot. He
cannot even open his eyes. The only sound is the hoarse rasp
of his breathing and the chattering of his teeth. Malaria is common enough on the kibbutz, but remains very dangerous in its
acute form. Golda turns to Regina:

"Go wake up Shimon!"

A few minutes later Regina and Golda are sitting in the
horse cart on either side of the sick man they have laid out

beneath the dark sky. Shimon is holding the reins. He is going as fast as he can, but the cart is swaying violently. Morris is oblivious. Wrapped in a blanket, he seems to have lost consciousness, the only sign of life his incessant shivering. Golda is holding him in her arms.

"He's out of danger for the moment," says the doctor at the hospital in Tiberiad, in the early morning light. "But you must understand one thing: he will not survive in a colony built at the edge of a swamp. He must leave Merhavia. And you must decide to do so right away, today. You have no choice. It is a matter of life or death."

2

ALBERT - 1923

The sun has just risen, the air is powdery. The Arab thoroughbreds seem heavy, as if fastened to the earth. Their sudden bursts of speed are therefore all the more impressive. In the shimmery light, in the scent of damp earth and dung, the lads, trainers, jockeys and stable boys move about to a precise and efficient choreography. A man is standing in their midst. In this country where all men have mustaches, he is clean-shaven. Standing at the edge of the racetrack, he is tranquil, taciturn, and never raises his voice. His fragility is imposing. With eager yet self-conscious respect, everyone calls him *khawâja* Albert, Monsieur Albert. He is in his thirties, of medium height, dressed in a linen suit and a white cloth cap that protects him from the low slant of sunlight and emphasizes the gentle set of the lower part of his face. There is something of the Levant in his black eyes and bushy eyebrows, his slow gestures, his long, elegant hands. He is at home here, among his horses.

Sitting a dozen yards or so farther along in the empty grandstand, a man has been watching him for some minutes. To judge by his physical aspect, he is a foreigner, in all likelihood an Englishman. Tall, with red hair, in tweeds, he has a long face and a lively eye. The horses surge by at a gallop and disappear. The man unfolds his legs, walks down the steep steps and goes up to Albert Pharaon:

"I'm terribly sorry, this is the only way I could find to meet you. My name is John Fillmore, I represent Barclays Bank for the Middle East."

"What can I do for you, Mr. Fillmore?"

"We would like to buy your bank in Haifa."

"Buy my bank?" asks Albert, turning for the first time to face his visitor.

"Barclays will be opening a branch in Jerusalem, and another one in Amman, in Transjordan. Your bank is firmly established in Haifa. To cover the north of Palestine, we would gain precious time if we could take over the bank, or at least participate in its capital."

"You don't seem worried about the political situation," murmurs Albert after a few moments of silence.

"Palestine has been so peaceful over the last two years that the British Empire is repatriating the majority of its troops. The challenge, now, is economic. The idea is to develop the country, the entire country. Banks and Western companies are moving in and opening branches with that aim in mind. And yet nothing is happening. Local banks aren't investing, except the Jewish banks."

"Jewish banks, Arab banks . . . How will you do business, Mr. Fillmore?"

"How can one do business without the support of the Arab bankers and businessmen, Mr. Pharaon?"

Fillmore likes the young banker's slow, direct rhythm. The almost painful attention with which he observes his horses seems to conceal a shyness, perhaps some personal difficulty.

"I fear that in Palestine," says Albert, "the idea of joint Judeo-Arab development is merely a dream on the part of the British Empire. I doubt whether it is feasible. The Jews want to conduct business only amongst themselves."

"One must invest, Mr. Pharaon, that you know. It requires an amount of energy that you do not have, and we are prepared to bring that to you."

It has been raining for over a week, and the sun will not have the time to dry the racetrack between now and tomorrow. Albert seems preoccupied.

"I won't sell my bank in Haifa."

"Might I inquire, Mr. Pharaon, whether you are Lebanese or Palestinian?"

"The reality is far more nebulous," replies Albert with a smile. "We used to move freely from one region to another before you and your French friends drew borders upon our territory."

"My offer is genuine, Mr. Pharaon."

"Call me Albert, please. Our Grand Prix will be run tomorrow morning. Why don't you come, you'll see the horses racing."

Off to one side, Albert perceives a figure in a blue dress walking toward him. He recognizes her from her walk: every one of her steps is filled with hesitation, with a desire to retreat. She sees that he is with someone and stops. Albert shakes John Fillmore's hand. The girl walks off to the side, to avoid meeting the visitor. Nina is beautiful, and doesn't know it. Very dark, tall, almost thin, her eyes are moist and searching, as if she were frightened. Her broad lips divide her face when she smiles. A woman's hips have suddenly grown on her child's body. She is only thirteen.

Albert makes as if to open his arms, then thinks better of it, and she understands his gesture. She goes up to him, touches him, and she can see he is content. He does not ask her why she isn't at school. He prefers not to know, he wouldn't know what to say to her. He takes her over to the track. The air is warm and humid. The mare is thirty yards away, flat out in a gallop, skimming the mud as she flies. Her brown coat is brilliant, glinting with light. This is Shaitane, with her gazelle-like neck and her massive body. She has the strength of a bull, yet uses it to achieve a floating lightness, her slender limbs giving her the stride of a dancer. Nina is in awe of this combination of vigor and grace, strength and vitality. Shaitane gallops toward her, hooves thundering menacingly. The young girl lets out a cry as the horse goes by.

"You got here just in time," says Albert with a laugh.

"She is magnificent!"

Nina is blushing. It is the sensual pleasure, the feeling of freedom that Shaitane has given her. Albert has always thought that his niece was the only member of his family who was truly alive.

The grandstand is overflowing with an unruly, insolent crowd; the rare women seem like islands amidst a flow of men. The place smells of pleasure and sweat. People are eating sunflower seeds, and husks litter the rows. It is the Sunday of the Grand Prix, and there's not a single empty seat. Strolling vendors shove their way by, stepping on feet, causing whistles, pinched arms, shouts. The ring of humanity circling the racetrack sways beneath a sky so brilliant that people are obliged to squint.

Albert Pharaon is in the first row, just in front of the official stand. With his binoculars he can see the shimmering picture of little boys in their open-necked shirts, of fathers herding their flocks of children, an entire working-class Beirut, people who live on another planet.

Shaitane comes at last onto the racetrack. He sees her quivering with impatience, snorting her strength through her nostrils. She rebels, steps sideways. The jockey holds her on a tight rein; he seems lighter than air. Albert sets his elbows on the guardrail. He has many horses. The only stable that can compare with his own belongs to his cousin Robert, a banker like himself. But it seems to Albert that no mare has ever affected him as much as this one.

Nina is by his right side, and touches his hand. The race has begun. Shaitane immediately takes the lead, no effort required as yet, only slightly ahead of the pack. Albert agreed with the jockey that she should be held back as long as possible—this does not seem an easy task. Aroused by the thoroughbreds running alongside her, by the dust and thunder of hooves, she is pulling at the bit holding her back. Through his binoculars Albert can see the froth forming at the corners of her mouth. The jockey has her under control. They have run the entire first lap and Shaitane is still in the lead. She has found her rhythm, and her pacing is perfect. In the penultimate turn, another horse suddenly threatens to block her off. To urge her to the side, the jockey uses his whip. She makes a sudden swerve to the side which throws her off and causes her to lose a few lengths. As they enter the final stretch, she has dropped back among the stragglers. And so it is at this point that she frees her stride: beneath the gaze of thousands of spectators, she shows her worth, passing her rivals one after the other. The crowd is on its feet. There is total silence. Shaitane hardly touches the ground, there is only one horse ahead of her now. She gains ground in the final furlongs, but not enough. A head behind: she comes second at the finish line. An "ooooh" of disappointment rises above the racetrack, immediately followed by a clamor of praise for her prowess.

Albert Pharaon has jumped to his feet like the rest of them. He shows no emotion. But his niece standing next to him notices that he is transfixed, utterly pale, gripping his hat in his hand. She bends her head and places it against his shoulder. He shapes his hat and, turning around, raises it slightly to greet his cousin Robert, whose horse has just won the Grand Prix.

In the racetrack's reception area, Robert Pharaon reigns as king of the day. Amidst the wood paneling, leather armchairs and hunting prints, he pours champagne for the privileged guests: high society people, government notables, the French High Commissioner and the representative of the British Empire, ladies in extravagant gowns, men in top hats, everyone who is anyone in Beirut. Most of the guests know one another, exchange smiles, despise each other. They raise their glasses to

the winning horse, but also to Shaitane. Sparkling gazes are
delighted by the rivalry between the two Pharaon cousins.

Albert seeks refuge with John Fillmore over by the French
windows. In such a stifling and brutal milieu, the English
banker draws stares. Under the pretext of exchanging com-
ments about the race, many people have come up to him to
make his acquaintance, and immediately buttonhole him on
British policy in the Middle East, on the consequences of the
Balfour declaration promising the Jews a homeland in Palestine, on immigration, on land acquisition, and all that sort of
thing.

"We've always gotten along with the Jews. They're the sons
of Arabs, just as we are."

"The ones from Europe, that's another story."

"What on earth got into you? Why the devil did Great
Britain have to go and promise a 'homeland' to the Jews in
Arab territory? I can't see how such a policy could serve your
interests."

"It's 'divide and rule.'"

"Divide who? The Jews don't make up ten per cent of the
inhabitants of Palestine. The British are endangering their relations with a very populous nation for the sake of a hypotheti-
cal future country."

John Fillmore merely smiles and nods. Those who are
speaking have no need of him to go on with their conversation.
Albert takes a moment to step back, and is intercepted from
behind by his sister Marcelle. She is a heavyset woman, wearing a white dress with ruffles; her husband, the marquis
Jacques de Kraym, is at her side, and she wants to be introduced to Fillmore. She always acts as if her brother owed her
something. She has never understood why Albert acts annoyed
with her. She has gotten used to it. But his close relation with
Nina, who is her daughter, drives her mad, once again. That
does not prevent her from being charmed by John Fillmore, or

from flashing her best smirking smile at him. Jacques de Kraym breaks into the conversation without hesitation:

"I'll tell you why Great Britain is conducting such an absurd policy in the Middle East. It is quite simply because the Jews are powerful and they have an occult power capable of forcing the mightiest nation on earth to act against its own interests."

"That's no more than an anti-Semitic cliché," says Albert Pharaon, emerging for the first time from his habitual reserve.

"How then do you explain such an enigma?" retorts Jacques de Kraym.

"I don't explain it. I have no idea."

In the midst of the hubbub, Albert's eyes seek to escape elsewhere. He catches sight of his niece, who seems bored all alone, leaning against the wall on the other side of the room. She turns around as if he had touched her. In her gaze he reads a hint of reproach, as if she were stifling. The gaze of a woman. He lifts his hand, a slight wave. She smiles back. Her face lights up, mischievous, childish once again.

"All I know," Jacques de Kraym is saying, raising his voice, "is that during the Great War the British promised the Arabs a great independent state to reward them for their support against the Turks. They even sent Lawrence to convince them. But no sooner was the war over than they forgot their promise for the sake of another one that they made to the Jews. So today the entire Arab nation is a victim of this treachery."

In the ensuing silence, all eyes are focused on Fillmore. He seems to show as little interest as ever. He takes the time to light his pipe and lets a moment go by before reacting:

"I have heard that you are a marquis, Monsieur de Kraym. I was unaware that there were titled citizens in the Middle East."

A current of silent jubilation flows through the small group of listeners. White-maned fathers promoting their grown sons, businessmen who acted as go-betweens for the Arab world with the West, prominent citizens sure of their power and masters of a country still feeling growing pains: such men love nothing more than a good row to assuage their boredom.

"Most of our aristocratic titles are Turkish," replies Jacques de Kraym, somewhat unsettled.

There is a slight commotion near the door. Irene has made her entrance. Her dress is a sort of transparent beige veil which does little to conceal her modest breasts. On her head is a hat with white feathers; she is a tiny woman and her high heels throw her off balance. Her lips are painted bright red. As she walks toward Albert with a malicious smile on her face, she is almost funny—like a clown delighting in her own appearance.

"Mr. Fillmore, allow me to introduce my wife, Irene."

The Englishman is briefly ruffled then, regaining his composure, he bends over and kisses Irene Pharaon's hand.

"So you are the famous John Fillmore!" she exclaims, her gaze unflinching.

"In person," he replies, lowering his eyes.

"We hear of no one but you, Mr. Fillmore. You've come here straight from London, or so I've heard. Where are you staying?"

"At the Saint-Georges."

"A relative of mine built it. He drew the arcades with his own hand, right onto the façade. I haven't had a chance to visit the rooms since the hotel opened. I've heard they are excellent."

"Indeed."

"Are you staying in Beirut for long?"

"I'm leaving tomorrow for Haifa."

"What a pity. Do come to see us this evening. We are receiving. You shall see, you shan't regret it."

Irene raises her champagne glass to propose a toast, but no longer knows to whom or to what. She giggles like a schoolgirl:

"I didn't mean to interrupt," she says, disingenuously. "Do

continue your conversation. What were you talking about? Tell me, Jacques."

"We were talking about politics," says Jacques de Kraym.

"About your title, to be exact," says Fillmore with a faint smile.

"There's not much to say. My father fell in love with an Austrian princess who could not marry him because he was a commoner. He belonged to a wealthy Christian family. So the Vatican granted him the title of 'papal marquis,' a distinction recognized by every court in Europe. Thus he was able to call himself Moussa *de* Kraym . . . and wed the princess, my mother."

"How extraordinary," says Fillmore.

"Jacques has not told you everything," adds Irene Pharaon. "When he was old enough to enter university, his mother objected to his studying to be a lawyer. The reason being, you see, that a marquis is not meant to work. She sent him to Paris with the order to spend as much money as he could. He started off with bridge, then went on to poker. And when he came back here, to the Levant, gambling remained his sole mistress. He is the pillar of the Beirut and Haifa circles, living off his income more magnificently than anyone I know. He owns entire villages. And he has one priceless quality: he knows how to lose."

Albert stops listening, disconnects. The flow of words may continue, but he no longer makes any effort to grasp their meaning. His appearance does not change, that of a perfectly educated man of the world. But deep within he is disgusted by the subterranean violence of these narrow circles—women stealing each other's husbands with a smile, little boys raped by priests, snide back-handed tricks, the reign of money, systems of allegiance, families . . . Even the two children he has with Irene: his feelings for them are only skin deep. Even as small toddlers they already belonged to an artificial world of governesses, propriety, and manners. He feels a warm flush on his cheeks. Why is he staying here? What is obliging him to stay here? His own passivity is stifling. Once again, he looks for his niece Nina, Nina de Kraym. But there is no one there now, where she had been standing.

3

MAY DAY - 1928

Morris Myerson has been watching his wife as she moves among the colored lanterns, political stands, red flags, and countless banners of the Histadrut.[1] Her simple white dress, tied at the waist, makes her look like a worker. Her body is lively and solid, but her step has become hesitant. She jumps at the shout of "Long live May Day!" booming down the megaphone as she passes, stops to listen to a few words of a faraway speech, then turns around at the first notes of a kibbutz song she used to hum. Her head, in constant motion, is like that of a bird on the look-out. Everything seems to intimidate her, whether it is the echo of the "Internationale" or patriotic verses declaimed in Yiddish. She wanders through the festivities as if transfixed. Even the sight of the workers eating with their families on the sunny lawns does not seem to be enough to warm her.

Despite her two pregnancies, she has become thinner. Her face has lost some of its roundness. As if her skin had grown drier, stretching the skin over her bones, emphasizing the power of her gaze. But Morris has to admit that some light has gone from her eyes. Golda's will is intact, that he knows, but her will has become mute, as if it has no purpose. He slips his arm around her waist. She turns to him and smiles:

"This is good, isn't it," he asks.

"Yes, it's good."

It was her idea to attend this May Day gathering in Herzlia.

[1] Jewish labor union.

She had talked about it that very morning, during breakfast: "We could leave Jerusalem around noon, go through Tel Aviv to leave the children at my sister's place, then go on just the two of us." Behind her practical tone of voice, Morris detected his wife's heavy sense of apprehension. In leaving the Merhavia kibbutz, she had left her political activity behind. Former comrades continued to come and visit her in Jerusalem, but she was no longer really up to date on what was happening. She had drawn a line and refused to look back. Today is the first time she has taken such a chance. Morris accompanies her on tiptoe, in the way a husband might accompany his wife to the home of a former lover, the very love of her life. Other couples are walking along the paths, arm in arm, but there are also groups of adolescents, large families, workers, intellectuals. The music and slogans bring them together with a shared feeling of belonging, and languages from all over the world can be heard. "To be Jewish is no longer a sign of distinction, since everyone here is Jewish," thinks Morris. "To introduce themselves, they are obliged to say they are Yemeni, Polish, Ukrainian, Russian, Lithuanian, German, Syrian . . . Palestine has allowed them to fulfill a deep fantasy, as deep as it is shameful: to stop being Jewish!"

Golda leaves his side and runs ahead. Perhaps she has seen something, or someone. Drawing closer, Morris finds himself at the edge of the central lawn. Golda turns around and with a movement of her head invites him to join her. He sees her smile, the smile of a child full of wonder but still somewhat reticent. A scattered crowd is listening to the speakers who succeed one another on the open air podium. Their words are fiery, but the general atmosphere is good-natured. People are listening with one ear from where they are sitting or lying on the grass; the sun is shining, they are happy. They are wearing their Sunday best, but from their fingernails you can see they are workers.

"It's you!"

Golda squints at the young woman, roughly her age, who has called out to her, a redhead with freckles, but she fails to recognize her.

"That's normal," replies the young woman. "I saw you at the kibbutz convention, almost four years ago. I didn't give a talk. My name is Esther Shapiro."

"May I introduce my husband, Morris Myerson."

"I booed you when you defended the nobility of household chores at the kibbutz. It seems so long ago! You went on talking while everyone was shouting, and in Yiddish."

"What are you doing now?" asks Golda.

"I've left the kibbutz. I'm working at the local Histadrut, in Herzlia. I also got married, and I have a little boy."

"And the kibbutz?"

"Whenever I miss it, I go back for a visit," she says brightly. "It's at Rishon le-Tsion, not far from here. Of course it's no longer the same thing. The kibbutz was the most fascinating experience of my life, but it's over with."

"Why?" insists Golda. Morris senses she is troubled, perhaps ill at ease.

"Because of the children," replies Esther. "I was watching them grow up year after year without a clearly defined father or mother. They didn't share any of our references, they were dealing with something completely unknown, people were expecting them to become some sort of New Man. I think I got frightened, quite simply."

"Frightened of what?"

"If the entire Jewish population of Palestine were living on a kibbutz, it would become common law. But in this case . . . it was something like a little laboratory. It felt as if we were turning our children into guinea pigs."

"If there is one new thing we've created in this country, on earth that is, one thing we can be proud of, now and forever,

that is the kibbutz. We've invented a radically different personal, social and emotional order, we've eliminated relations of
power between people, and abolished feelings of ownership
and competition. Not only for ourselves, but also for our children, from the moment of their birth!"

"You've kept your faith," says Esther, laughing.

"Yes," replies Golda with a stern smile.

"And you, what has become of you?"

"Me? At the moment I'm living in Jerusalem . . . "

Morris feels her fleeting glance go straight to his heart. He
wonders what else she will say, but she doesn't have the time.
A man rushes up to them and takes her warmly by the arm. She
is startled, blushes. David Remez is the boss of Solel Boneh,
the company that builds the roads, bridges and houses for the
entire Yishuv. He is also the man who had come to sit beside
her at the kibbutz convention. All night they had had to refrain
from falling into each other's arms.

"How long has it been," he says, still holding her arm, "four
years?"

" . . . and five months."

She watches as he shakes Morris's hand and greets Esther.
His deep-set black eyes, rectangular face and severe mustache
give him an aristocratic air. But all he needs is to smile—something he does not do often—to become the most accessible of
men. He threads his arm through Golda's and leads her away.
She has the impression that there is a time lag in her responses
to his eager questions, to his scarcely concealed interest in her.

"What's wrong, Golda?" he asks after a silence.

"I'm all right. I'm still working for Solel Boneh in Jerusalem,
that job you found for me. I'm also teaching English in a private school. Morris is still working at the library . . . "

"And so?"

"Nothing, it's just that . . . "

She sighs, she can't say more. Suddenly over the loudspeaker comes a strong, magnetic, velvety voice, one of those rare voices which speaks to you in person and obliges you to listen.

"Jean Jaurès, who defended Dreyfus, said that to go from a republican democracy to a socialist democracy, the only way is to reinforce the working classes."

The voice pauses and the words remain suspended, as if this were the first proposition of a future enigma.

"Therefore what we say is that in order to transform a nation of shopkeepers and intellectuals into an independent nation, the only solution is to create a mass of workers! That means that we too must, as a nation, transform ourselves into workers cultivating the land, living off the land, developing our industry with our own hands. In such a way that the working class becomes a nation of workers, for only such a nation will be capable of leading the transformation which is essential to our national rebirth!"

Men and women start to get to their feet, to see who the new speaker might be. David leans close to Golda's ear:

"It's Zalman Shazar, you must know him. My best friend."

"I've never seen him," she replies, disconcerted. "I didn't imagine him like that."

A pointed face, a mustache forming two small hooks at the corner of his mouth, silver-rimmed oval glasses: there is nothing particularly striking about Shazar—unless it is his way of moving like a dancer. The only distinctive thing is his *rubashka*, a high-collared shirt from Eastern Europe, buttoned on the side and very familiar to Golda.

"I know no one as obsessed as he is," adds David. "He edits the *Davar* newspaper, which he founded; and he's translated Rachel de Kinnereth. I'm sure you'll like him."

"Rachel de Kinnereth is my favorite poet," murmurs Golda.

"I've heard that they were lovers," says Esther.

On hearing her words Golda feels a pang in her heart. How long has she been thirsting for this? These two men, showing

up at the same time, Zalman like a tightrope walker, David a
pillar: they are like one person to her. Two poles of the same
magnet, so to speak.

"But are we a nation?" booms Zalman Shazar. "Not even a
tribe! I am a product of Exile. I was born captive to fear, to the
bent back, to a host of desires. I only truly saw the light when
I decided, in Minsk, to create self-defense committees against
pogroms. This was not part of the Jewish tradition—the tradition of exile, I mean. To break with that tradition, we had to
assimilate the idea that the aggression we were being subjected
to was intolerable—and that it should no longer be tolerated,
therefore. And your presence here today, in this country which
is yours, is the most brilliant proof of that idea!"

There is a burst of applause amidst the silence. The speaker
raises his hands to ask for calm, as if he needed to concentrate
in order to think and make others think. David and Golda
move together toward the podium, leading Morris and Esther
behind them. They pause when the crowd becomes too dense.
Everyone is on their feet now, and the echo of Zalman Shazar's
voice has begun to draw those who were strolling along the
adjacent paths.

"Today, we are no longer living in someone else's country,
and we don't need to ask anyone for permission to live. On the
contrary, we are asserting our right to *return* to the country of
our ancestors, to settle here, to cultivate the land and develop
the resources, without constraint. We are not strangers in this
land, but the descendants of those who ruled here in the past.
We have come back here to settle, and it's as if we were all born
here!"

His words are met with a thunder of applause, but something
holds Golda back. Her throat tightens even more. Only now does
she admit to herself that Zalman is handsome. He is whirling on
the stage, his body and soul are one. She is overcome by physical
emotion, and unspeakable sadness at the same time. David's gaze

is upon her, his brow inclined toward her, his stare coming from deep within. Zalman hammers his ideas home:

"Because we haven't come back here just for our own sake, as private individuals; we have come back here as a collective nation!"

The ovation starts again, surges, and yet again the speaker's hands try to discourage them; he is determined to have his say.

"We have been chosen among all nations to bear witness to one God. But we had doubted Him and He condemned us to two thousand years of diaspora, the *Galut*, the form of exile reserved for Israel. Other nations may simply dream of their place of birth. But for us Jews, our roots are in God and in the land that He chose for us. That is why our return to Zion is not simply a material return, but also a spiritual return. And if you have any doubts, go to the Wailing Wall in Jerusalem. Stay there for a moment, for a long moment, facing this last vestige of King Solomon's temple. And then not only will you see, you will feel with all your being the secret of the long life of our people. Because we are one people!"

He ignores the ensuing clamor, does not even hear it. He is in his element, moving from one subject to another, from poetry to politics, from nationalism to socialism, from secularism to mysticism. Everyone hears and recognizes the associations behind his wandering discourse. He does not harangue the crowd with the words pouring from his lips, but with his arms and legs, his shoulders and knees, his entire body. Suddenly he is talking to his fist, and then his fingers. He paces to and fro, turns his back to the audience, turns again to face them, leans against the wall, without ever interrupting his endless monologue. Golda has the impression that even his bones are talking. Talking? They are shouting, raging, exhorting, imploring. His body goes into a trance, whirls in a spiral, a syncopated dance which the young woman, awestruck, immediately recognizes for what it is: a Hasidic dance.

4

Jerusalem - Tel Aviv - 1928

The faces seem to be coming toward her, but it is she who is going toward them. She weaves her way through the crowds in the winding narrow Arab souk, among the scent of spices, and sets off again through the narrow alleys between the streets. Only a general sense of direction is important to her. She is running, like someone who no longer knows what to do. The Wailing Wall is suddenly there before her. The street is so narrow that she is obliged to step back and raise her eyes to look at it from the side. She has never given a damn about old stones, and does not count religious Jews among her friends. They have been living in this city for so long that they have accepted certain compromises. The two most sacred mosques overlook the Wall, and the Holy Sepulcher is three hundred yards from there. Together the three religions weigh on the shoulders of Jerusalem, and Golda is not even a believer. But she is short of breath, and her heart is pounding.

She moves forward and places her right palm against the stone. It is warm. An old woman in tears inserts a carefully folded piece of paper between the stones, a plea or a dream addressed to God, a *kvitlach*. There are thousands of them in the Wall. Since time immemorial Jews have been coming here to lament the destruction of the temple and the dispersal of their people. Wrapped in his ritual shawl, a young man is praying, banging his forehead against the stone. Golda watches as he loses all self-control. His body is in a trance, he contorts himself, his torso rocks back and forth, his head is thrown back, his

eyes roll in their sockets. He is dancing with an extreme violence, as if he wanted to be rid of his limbs. A higher force
seems to inhabit his body and he wriggles desperately to try and
rid himself of it. He is no longer *separate.* He and the wall are
one, in a frenzied culmination, an organic fusion.

David realizes he has had nothing to eat since noon the day
before. Even the fact of finding himself in his office in the Histadrut headquarters—overwhelmed with papers that are perfectly ordered in his mind—comes as a surprise. He worked
until five o'clock in the morning, fell asleep on the sofa right
there behind him, and woke at eight to pick up his work where
he had left it. Night and day are words that no longer have a
great deal of meaning for him. His life is a continuum of time,
interrupted now and again by a few hours of sleep. He decides
to go and eat something. Walking head down along the busy
corridors of the Histadrut, he hurries down the stairs toward
the entrance. In the street he is met by a flash of lightning
immediately followed by a deafening thunderclap. Even before
he leaves the entrance to the building, hailstones big as chick-
peas begin to rain down. Bent to the storm, an old woman protects her head with a piece of soaked woolen cloth, then comes
for shelter under the same canopy. She puts down her pack-
ages, raises her eyes to look at him and gives a start. He too
gives a start: it is Golda. She has changed so much in two
weeks, he cannot believe it.

"What's happened to you, Golda?"

Her lips are trembling, she cannot utter a sound. He puts his
arms around her. With a shudder, she hides in his neck.

"Golda, what is it?" he asks again.

"I just have to . . . get the bus back to Jerusalem."

"Forget that. Speak to me. You looked so well the last time
I saw you."

"It was precisely that meeting, on the first of May . . . "

She is unable to say more, her tears overwhelm her and she is helpless. Remez is stunned. The strong, vibrant young woman full of promise that he met in Degania seems to have lost any trace of self-confidence. She seems so weary, so desperate and drained.

"Listen," he says in a hushed voice. "Let's go to the café. You must tell me."

She is too exhausted to resist. She reaches down for her parcels, Remez picks them up for her. He takes her arm and they make their way like that down the middle of the sidewalk. In the café they choose a secluded table. Golda's words are like tears: she can no longer hold them back.

"All these years, David, I swear, I tried everything, I really tried. I forced myself to look after Morris and to love him the way he deserved to be loved, I gave him two children, I was running from morning to night, kept the house, worked hard . . . I couldn't cope, no one can, there's such poverty, but it was my duty, good mother, good wife, a relentless struggle, for four whole years! I became an expert on poverty, but it didn't stop us from being famished. I remember bursting into tears one day simply because we had no more money to buy some lamp oil. Can you imagine?"

"I cannot understand why you let yourself be closed off like that without fighting back."

"Is that what it means to be a Zionist?" she says with a sad smile. "To come to Palestine, to be happy simply to be here and, yes, to suffer . . . I let the weeks go by one after the other. I thought I was getting used to it, that I would end up getting used to it."

"Why didn't you come and see me?"

"To say what? That life is difficult? It was even more difficult in Merhavia. But there, something else kept us going."

"Maybe you were made for life on the kibbutz."

"That's what I thought too. Two years ago, when Menahem

was six months old, I decided to go back with him to Merhavia
to live. I was so unhappy that Morris let us go. But even the
kibbutz had changed: the swamp had been drained, there were
eucalyptus trees everywhere, lawns . . . I wanted to go back
there to work the land, and they gave me the nursery—nine
children to raise, including my own. I began to miss Morris
more than I would have thought. I lasted six months. When I
came back to Jerusalem with my little boy, Morris was so
happy! He thought I'd just been going through a crisis and
that now at last we would be happy. A month later I was preg-
nant with Sarah. I hadn't realized that two small children at
home is not the same as one small child. I had to leave Menahem with neighbors and take the baby with me to the school
where I am teaching. Only a few weeks after Sarah's birth I was
suffocating again. It was too late to change my mind again. I
thought I'd be able to resign myself to it. But then there was
May Day, and your friend Zalman ruined everything."

"Zalman?"

"What he said that day broke my heart. He showed me that
the life I've dreamt of is possible, and he opened all my old
wounds. Yesterday I followed the advice he was giving the
crowd: I went to the Wall. I don't believe in God. But the Wall
is alive. I can talk to it, listen to it, have a relation with it. This
Wall is like a fortress that has been safeguarding the land for
the Jews' return."

Remez takes Golda's hand across the table. She lowers her
gaze, to hide her tears:

"Oh, David! I don't know what to do anymore, I literally
can't take it anymore! I didn't come to Eretz Israel for this!"

The waitress comes with their order. This gives them a
moment to breathe. They wait in silence while she puts down
the plates and drinks.

"Listen," says Remez. "You have to see that you have been
forcing yourself to make a superhuman effort, an inhuman

effort, to turn away from your true vocation. That is where your pain is coming from. And that pain doesn't help a thing, doesn't lead anywhere. I spend my days fixing problems that are complicated in their own way. My method is simple. I put the emotional aspect to one side and make a cold evaluation of the difficulty, and how I can respond to it."

"Since you know, then tell me how to deal with this!"

"I'm not the one who knows, you are. You are allowing yourself to be blinded by your feelings, your children, your husband, your guilt . . . "

"What are you trying to say?"

"That for four years you've been wasting your time. The life you've desperately been trying to live in Jerusalem is not your own. You have to stop this waste."

"But how?"

"To begin with, stop putting yourself down. You have a rare talent, Golda, exactly the kind that the Zionist movement needs. For weeks I've been looking for someone who could take charge of a certain task . . . "

"What task?" she asks eagerly.

"Right here, at the Histadrut headquarters in Tel Aviv. We need someone to set up farm schools in order to teach agriculture to young women. Times have changed. There are fewer immigrants and the *yishuv* is getting more and more women on their own, who are motivated but inexperienced. They make it a point of honor to do all the jobs which are normally reserved for men, including paving the roads. The problem is that they have no training and they don't know how to get organized or how to live together. In fact, no one knows."

"That would be wonderful!" says Golda, her eyes suddenly shining. "But I'd have to live in Tel Aviv."

"It's imperative. The Histadrut would find you an apartment in the neighborhood where we all live. You'll see, you'll be fine. No point in hiding it: we all hate Jerusalem and its clerics. They don't care for us and we return it in kind. Tel Aviv is our town, our neighborhood, our familiar ghetto."

"But how can I? Morris, the children . . . "

"Don't dramatize," says Remez, somewhat harshly. "Most of the leaders of the Histadrut or of the party have a family and children too. That doesn't stop them from working. And your kids can come and live with you. Your sister lives in Tel Aviv, she'll help you look after them and bring them up. For the rest, I don't know you very well yet. But what you have inside you is stronger than you are, Golda Myerson. It's time for you to decide what you want to do with your life."

5

BEIRUT - HAIFA - 1928

She knocks and no one answers. The house behind the sculpted door seems to be sleeping. She knocks again. The echo is that of a huge empty cavern. She looks up at the windows. The day is soft and clear, the air saturated with light. Behind her, the lawns and groves are perfectly trimmed. Everything is in order, except for her. Tears well in her eyes. She knocks harder still. A faint sound, she thinks she's heard a faint sound inside. She listens. Someone is coming to the door. Leaning on her cane, Mireille, Irene Pharaon's mother, opens for her:

"Nina, lovely Nina!"

The compliment pierces her to the heart. For some time now, everyone has been saying this to her. It's true that she has grown, that her tall and slender body has filled out and taken on a suppleness that draws gazes. But these gazes do not flatter her, they bother her. She does not like herself, she does not feel beautiful. At the age of seventeen and a half, all she wants is to be left alone. But even this request, this prayer, the childish anger that everyone can read in her eyes, leaves her more attractive than ever. What can she do? She leans against the doorway. The crickets hidden in the umbrella pines of the garden are coming to life, and their seesaw chorus makes her feel dizzy. Her arms full of books, she tries to speak normally, but her lips are trembling. Mireille is smiling in the way only deaf people know how to smile:

"What? What did you say? Speak up!"

"I am asking whether Uncle Albert is there!" shouts Nina, close to releasing the sob which is lodged in her throat.

"I really cannot hear a thing. Do come in. I'll go fetch my ear trumpet."

Reluctantly she follows the old woman into the house. A twilight darkness reigns, all the curtains are drawn. Empty bottles of alcohol, dirty glasses, playing cards left tossed on the green carpet . . . Clearly, the servants have not yet done their rounds. And yet it is nearly noon. Mireille has gone to look for her trumpet. Nina notices two men sound asleep on the large living room sofa. She steps back, knocks over a pedestal table.

"Who's there?"

The young woman raises her eyes. Leaning over the balustrade, Irene Pharaon is watching her. She is still in her nightdress.

"It's only me, Aunt Irene," says Nina softly.

"I see it's you, Nina. What do you want?"

"I want to know if Uncle Albert is here."

"Albert? Not at all. He's away . . . he's always away."

"In Haifa?"

She calculates that she has enough money on her to pay for the trip in a collective taxi. She can be in Haifa in three hours.

"No, he got back from Haifa last night, and left again this morning . . . Just a moment . . . For Geneva? For London? I can't remember. Somewhere in Europe, at any rate. He said he'd be gone for ten days or so."

"There we go, I've got it!" says Mireille, coming back to the living room, waving her trumpet. "What were you saying?"

Nina doesn't even have the strength left to open her mouth. From the first floor, Irene shouts, "What time is it? Nina, are you hungry? Wait a moment, I'll be right down. Where are you going? Nina!"

She walks through the city. One step after the other. She already came this direction, from the lycée. Now she's drifting.

She sets off in another direction, down streets she's never taken. She is not sure how she arrives at the corniche which runs along the sea. The wind is heavy with salt, and it sticks to her face, dries on her lips. She keeps walking, keeps herself from crying. If Albert had been here, he would have known what to do. He would have dropped everything for her, he would have offered her an arm to lean on. She has no one. A whirlwind is pulling at her feet. She is struggling with all her strength, and at the same time she is letting herself go. She feels a strange complicity with what is happening to her. Something inside her. Her body belongs to her, that is something she has always believed. And now she realizes that her body is still part of her family. She has been handed over, and she is relenting, passively. It disgusts her. If he had wanted, she would have left with Albert. But that is not something he wants, or can think of wanting. She is crying. When she raises her eyes, she notices that she is outside Arouss el-Bahr, the Bride of the Sea, a popular café at the foot of the lighthouse. She goes in. It is big, and there are wooden tables outside. There is no one. She sits down, orders a tea. She has known happy times in this café, she used to come with her girlfriends. Entire afternoons, talking, laughing. Her thoughts overwhelm her, she stops them from unfolding. She struggles to live in the present moment. The tea, too sweet, spreads its heat through her belly. She watches the waves breaking against the rocks, concentrates on them, tries to give herself to their ebb and flow. To no avail. She cannot make herself cease to exist.

It is seven in the evening when she pushes the door to her home. The sound of conversation emerges from the kitchen. The dining room is lit up, the table is set. There are flowers. No one in the living room. She seizes the moment to creep up to her room. She closes the door. On her bed lies her sexiest dress, the one with the low-cut neckline.

*

The car moves slowly along the corniche, deserted on this early Sunday morning. The seats are leather, the seascape takes on a curious hue through the smoked glass windows. The particular light of Beirut, the coast, the smell of the sea, all chart a familiar geography which Albert Pharaon rediscovers with pleasure. Whatever he might say to the contrary, he cannot deny the feeling of release each time he comes back. And yet he does like Europe. He has just spent two weeks there. All the business he had to deal with has been dealt with. But once everything had been taken care of, his longing for the Levant returned. To be honest, he is in his element neither here nor there. He lives somewhere in between. For the last four years the solution to this problem has been a constant coming and going.

The car leaves the corniche and heads for the hills above the city. Everyone must still be sleeping this early in the morning. He can stop by the house, get changed, and go to the stables without running into anyone. Hanna stops the car at the foot of the double stairway leading up to the front entrance.

"I'll need you in half an hour," says Albert before climbing the steps.

The chauffeur sees to the suitcases then comes back to wait by the car. He doesn't even have time to light a cigarette; Albert suddenly rushes back out. This is no longer the same man. Pale, agitated, his jaw clenched, he shoves Hanna, who was opening the rear door for him, out of the way, then slides in behind the wheel, and roars off.

"Albert, what a surprise! So early in the morning! I thought you were in Milan . . . or Zurich, I can't keep track . . . "

"Don't play with me, Marcelle. Where is Nina?"

Brother and sister know each other too well. Everything is a convention between them, even their anger, even their combat rituals. As she has been roused from her bed, Marcelle de Kraym shows that she is ready for battle:

"What a way to behave! You come back from your trip, you run over here, you don't even say hello . . . I thought you were more worldly than that. What is wrong with you, my poor Albert?"

"This is what is wrong with me!"

He tosses the invitation into her face: "The marquis Jacques de Kraym and Madame de Kraym have the pleasure of inviting you to the marriage of their daughter Nina . . . " Marcel snatches at the invitation. Her laugh is triumphant.

"Is this what is bothering you? But my dear brother, it's not as if it were happening to you! I thought you'd come here to congratulate me!"

Albert is not in the mood to endure her sarcasm. There is no longer anything nonchalant about his stance. He has suddenly become the incarnation of the landowning dynasty to which he belongs, the descendent of generations of masters who are used to being obeyed. He asks Marcelle curtly why she has sold off her daughter, and at what price. With a smile on her face, Nina's mother resists. Power and fortune flow in her veins too. The fiancé? A *ricchissimo* Egyptian, who will take his wife to live in Cairo. How old? Thirty-six, yes, more than twice Nina's age, and so what? Albert would like to see his niece? Not a chance! She has gone, vanished; he has come too late. Where is she? In the mountains somewhere, in a safe place where there is no chance he will find her.

"You've imprisoned her!" he says, white with anger.

"Don't be ridiculous, Albert. I know you. I've sent her to a safe place to keep you from ruining her future. She'll dry her tears, your little sweetheart . . . Who do you think she is? A poor innocent child? Honestly. A little girl who doesn't understand what is happening? You are blind, my dear Albert, and she is the one who's made you blind! Don't worry about her, I know her better than you do. She's my daughter; she's hard."

"You don't know her. You've never even looked at her."

"What business is it of yours, anyway? Do you even understand what is going on? The marquis de Kraym is marrying off his daughter, and he's inviting all the high society in Lebanon and Palestine to the ceremony. You'll see with your own eyes: they will all be there. And why not? It is true that Jacques has been close to ruin . . . but only close. Believe me if you can: in a few years, he has lost the thirty-seven villages he owns in Palestine, and all the surrounding land. He would never have been able to make and squander so many liquid assets if the Jews didn't pay cash, top dollar. Even if we had sold everything—shares, houses, the yacht, the horses—it wouldn't have been enough to cover his debts. Jacques has never worked. What were we supposed to do? We were threatened with being thrown out of the world, do you understand? Out of the world!"

Albert pulls himself together. He has realized that his brother-in-law is in the type of situation where the only solution is to speak to Marcelle as a businessman.

"How much do you want to call off the whole thing?"

"Your fortune wouldn't be enough," she retorts. "What would be the point of seeing both my husband and my brother ruined at the same time? Anyway, I have no desire to spend the rest of my days hearing how you, Albert, were the one who saved us."

"You would rather it were the Egyptian?"

"He has been unbelievably generous. He negotiated a moratorium on the debts, and got us off so we only paid a fraction. And in addition, he has laid out a staggering amount of money, never mind what he will have to pay later on. Which all goes to show how much he cares for Nina."

"An excellent transaction, in other words."

"Don't make fun of me!" shouts Marcelle, showing her claws. "What's wrong with that? Marriages have always been there for that very reason. It's part of the game. Jacques gets to come back into the world. So it goes. Nothing new. Do you think anyone is worried about Nina? No one, apart from you. So stop worrying and everything will be fine. Next time you see her she'll be wearing a white gown, she'll be radiant, outside the entrance to the cathedral on her fiancé's arm."

"I just want to hear, from her lips, that she said yes. That is all I ask."

"You ask? In whose name? She is still a minor, and by law she is subject to the authority of her parents. You have no power over her. You are neither her father, nor her brother, nor her fiancé. But I can see that you are very upset . . . I am beginning to wonder."

"Wonder about what?"

"Don't play naïve with me. I don't know exactly what the two of you have been up to, but it's obvious you're besotted with her. Clear as day. I'm very sorry for you: you won't be the first person to screw her."

Albert Pharaon is thunderstruck. He grows pale, his arms waving helplessly in a gesture of stupefaction and dismay. It is too much for him. With both hands he grabs hold of a vase, lifts it and smashes it at his sister's feet. The servants come running from all quarters. Standing in the midst of the debris, Marcelle shouts,

"So it's true! You'd set your heart on my little girl! What sort of unnatural uncle are you?! I was right! At last you've shown your true face! What right do you think you have to pretend to uphold the law? Did you marry for love? Are you happy with your wife? Or your children? You stroll across the drawing room with your nose turned up, but you're just like us, exactly. The same lifestyle, the same failings. You belong to this world—our world, with every bone in your body. You think that just because you don't play cards you've been saved? You think you're above all that? But your roulette, your sleazy hang-out, is the racetrack! My poor friend. You spend a fortune to buy a thoroughbred horse who, it turns out, can hardly finish the race. You gamble, and you lose. Just like us. And you start over. Just like us. Nina doesn't belong to you, she will never belong to you! And now, get out, I don't want to see you anymore."

It is eleven in the morning when Albert Pharaon opens his front door. He has just spent two long hours with his horses. He is very calm now. Everyone is asleep. He sits down at his desk and signs some papers.

"Marwan, I'm leaving this morning. My suitcases haven't been unpacked yet, just transfer them to the Bentley. Hanna will drive me to Haifa. He'll bring the car back and leave it here."

"Is there anything I must tell Madame Irene?"

"Nothing. Only that I've left."

"Will you be here for your niece's wedding next Saturday?"

"This document is the title deed to Shaitane; I've made it over in Nina's name. Give it to her with this letter. I'm counting on you."

Old Marwan's voice suddenly grows hoarse:

"But, but Monsieur Albert . . . won't I see you again?"

6

THE PINK HOUSE - 1929

C linging to the hillside, the city of Haifa faces the sky above and the bay below. Villas occupy the heights, middle-class homes the middle level, and the lower town, around the port, is made up of the working-class neighborhoods. Each bend in the road along the winding road from the summit signals a change of social class. The Pharaon villa, identifiable from its pink stones, is located near the summit, on its own between two levels. The impression it gives of being suspended in a luxurious nowhere suits Albert perfectly. His field of vision is filled largely with the sky, and with the sea at the foot of a vertiginous drop below; the infrequent clouds are his closest neighbors. From the circular balcony on the second floor he is absent-mindedly contemplating his abandoned garden, the octagonal pond with its brackish water, and beyond, the magnificent void. He is waiting for the slow dropping of the sun to the horizon, the progressive shifting of light. This is all he expects. Nothing in his social life is appealing enough to lure him away from this gentle idleness. He tries to keep up with the political news: it serves as a background, a vague, repetitive murmur. All he asks is to be left alone. Not forever, no doubt, but for a time. As if he were in convalescence, or following a treatment for alcoholism.

Najjar, clothed in a white jellaba, brings him the afternoon papers, then vanishes soundlessly. Albert has disposed of all the staff at the Pink House except for Najjar. The son of an Egyptian who was in service to the Pharaon family for his entire life, the young man suddenly found himself alone and in charge, and this has made a great impression on him. His eyes glow with a devotion he expresses by trying never to disturb his master, gliding from room to room like a ghost. Albert appreciates him for it, and for his loyalty, his light touch, his discretion.

He leafs through the newspapers; nothing interests him. Basically, he never really decided to leave Beirut to live alone. His niece's forced marriage has merely made him aware of the disgust he feels for his own existence. He was incapable of wearing the mask required to attend the pretense of a wedding, so in a way he left because it was impossible to do otherwise. Nina's image was haunting him. He imagined the young woman, scarcely out of her adolescence and already sold off, in Cairo. He was sickened by the fact that he had not been able to help her, and the idea of associating with the same circles that had handed her over made his hackles rise. He went back to Lebanon two weeks later, only to leave again at once. He no longer knew how to behave, he couldn't cope. In Haifa he feels as if he is working, because he is meeting with the directors of his bank. But he loves this town, so new and diverse that no one can really claim to be a native. In Beirut, his horses took up more of his time than his children. His son and daughter are growing up without him, all aspects of their life are taken care of. They are strangers to him, and the vague desire he has had to grow closer to them has not changed a thing. As for Irene, she did not realize at first that he was leaving for good. When she did realize, her reaction was to compose astonishing love letters to him which, utterly perplexed, he received in Haifa. She was playing at the woman in love who is abandoned, and she ended up believing it. Albert accepted his allotted role, that of the man who runs away. His visits to Beirut became increasingly infrequent. But his concern for appearances had not yet disappeared entirely. Beneath his nonchalance, some cowardice remained. If he had been freer, he would have asked for a divorce. Instead, he is hiding between sky and sea. As a refuge, it is ideal. His life there is solitary and sensual, a heady immobility.

"Najjar, I won't be dining in this evening."

Surprised, the young servant pauses. This evening there will be a reception in Jerusalem for the King of England's birthday, and Albert would like to accept the invitation. After weeks of solitude, he is curious: how will it feel to be brutally projected into the world, onto the stage, even if it is only for one night?

7

THE KING'S BIRTHDAY - 1929

T hree automobiles are winding their way up the pine-fringed road. Golda is sitting in the rear of the second one. The heady scent of the garrigue drifts in through the open windows. Her four years of domestic confinement have left her famished, and it is that hunger that has driven her to be where she is tonight. Zalman Shazar is sitting to her right, David Remez to her left. David has kept all his promises; he got her settled, introduced her. She could have fallen into his arms, and he had sensed as much. But he was taking his time, he knew the moment would come. His friend Zalman beat him to it. He is the one who gave Golda the strength to leave her family life, and he is the one who has possessed her. She owed that much to him, she loves his poetry. But she has not cut herself off from others. In love, too, her appetite is voracious. In the midst of this virile company, with their casual, coarse relations, she has managed to make herself accepted, without closing any doors behind her.

The automobiles come to a halt outside Government House. The brilliantly lit building of the High Commission stands out against the late afternoon sky. They step out of their cars: David Ben Gurion, Isaac Ben Zvi, Moshe Sharett, David Remez, Zalman Shazar, Levi Eshkol, Haim Arlosoroff, their assistants and their bodyguards. Golda is their interpreter. They all live in the same neighborhood in Tel Aviv, and spend all their time with each other, remaking the world—and Palestine in particular. For them this garden party is no mere social event, but a foray onto a battleground, where they must be seen, and face the enemy.

The King's Birthday has always been a moving occasion for Lord Herbert Charles Plumer. Whether the celebration is held in Malta, Rhodesia or Jerusalem does not make a great deal of difference: a High Commissioner is always standing on a piece of Great Britain. Completely at ease in his white uniform, he welcomes his guests with Lady Plumer, the love of his life, at his side. Both of them savor this unchanging déjà-vu. To a background music of bagpipes played by the Seaforth High-landers, the same costumes and uniforms parade across the lawn—local dignitaries, elegant women in their gauzy dresses, teachers and missionaries—British colonial society, a little world divided into clans, graduates of Oxford or Cambridge, with their passion for cricket or polo, all gathered to pay homage to their beloved sovereign.

Plumer was a formidable warrior, a hero of the Great War. But the war is over, he has no more ambitions, his career is nearing its end. He is happy in Palestine, and intends to remain so. From the very first day he has asked his district commissioners to stop bringing him their daily briefs: "There is no political situation, so don't go making one!"

"Look at them," says Oussama to Albert. "You can stare all you like. For them, we are transparent."

The British guests are indeed speaking only to other British guests. Only those officials whose job it is to be in contact with the *natives* welcome the Jewish and Arab guests.

"That stunning woman with the mother-of-pearl fan in her hand is Annie Landau," he continues. "She is more English than the English and more Jewish than the Zionists."

Oussama is director of the Barclays Bank in Haifa, but he looks nothing like a banker. He belongs to Jerusalem's leading family—the leading family in all of Palestine, in other words.

But he does not care about his own family or anyone else's for that matter. He is the *enfant terrible* of the Husseini clan, and all that matters to him is his own pleasure. His escapades inspired his family to find him a job in Haifa, any job, provided it take him away from Jerusalem. His outspokenness has earned him the enmity of most—and Albert's friendship. Albert feels like he is at the theatre; the oblique light changes colors and makes things seem unreal. At the foot of the monumental residence, the lawn seems to be moving. Soldiers in red tunics mark out the vast space criss-crossed by an army of waiters.

There is agitation in the crowd over by the garden gates. Accompanied by a numerous suite, Oussama's uncle, Hadj Amin el-Husseini, the grand mufti of Jerusalem, has arrived in full regalia, jellaba and white cloak. He is only thirty-three, but his stature and the fire in his eyes are proof of a natural strength tempered by the exercise of power. Lord and Lady Plumer go down the steps from the porch to greet their most distinguished Arab guest. Hadj Amin's smile is surprisingly charming.

"He always goes about with an invisible network of loyal, influential people," says Oussama. "Uncles, cousins, nephews . . . They're all here, and they're all sold to the British. Not a single one of them takes any notice of me. When they do happen to come across me, it's as if there were a hole in their vision. They are convinced that they are the natural leaders of Palestinian society. But in fact it is the rival family, the Nashashibis, who have just won the elections. When the first British High Commissioner appointed my uncle grand mufti, he immediately offered the City Hall of Jerusalem to Ragheb el-Nashashibi. In buying the two rival families—and all the others who depend on them directly or indirectly—the British have a hold on both the Palestinian 'power' and their 'opposition.' That is why for years the country has been at peace. The

British impose their rule in the same way in the four corners of the Empire. But the difference here is the Jews!"

The man leading the Jewish delegation is short and sturdily built, his black hair smooth against a broad forehead, and he is very shabbily dressed. His ribcage seems about to burst the buttons of his jacket, and his poorly ironed shirt stays closed thanks merely to the crooked knot of his necktie. And yet there is no disputing the impression of compact and concentrated strength he exudes. "He looks like a bulldog . . . or a bull," thinks Albert, recognizing Ben Gurion; he has often seen his photograph in the papers. The group of people with him—half a dozen men and one woman—are as badly dressed as he is. Far from acting self-conscious, they are full of confidence. Lord and Lady Plumer turn to Ben Gurion, making an effort to display exactly the same amount of warmth and friendliness that they had shown a few minutes earlier to Hadj Amin el-Husseini. The High Commissioner hurries up to the Arab dignitary who was on the verge of slipping away, then spreads his arms and invites the two opposing camps to shake hands, which they do reluctantly, to the applause of the crowd of guests.

"There you have the British fantasy," whispers Oussama. "This handshake will be on the front pages of all the papers tomorrow."

The British guests and their wives surround Hadj Amin and his followers. For them he represents the East—exoticism and that faint whiff of despotism which they have come to find. All the Biblical images they have in mind—shepherds dressed as in the time of Abraham, palm trees, dunes, camel caravans: that is something the Arabs embody. But none of them gather around Ben Gurion and his followers. The British may be favorable to Zionism in London, but in Jerusalem the Jews make them feel ill at ease. Their impression is that the Jews are merely paying lip service to British authority.

"The Arabs may be charmers," says Oussama, "but deep down they are submissive and *sympathiques* . . . They make good subjects. 'At least the Arabs are glad to see us,' said a British officer to me one day when he was complaining about the harshness of the Jews. And he went on to add: 'The English who come to Palestine are more or less pro-Jewish when they arrive, then after a while they become pro-Arab, and they invariably end up pro-British.'"

Oussama points out the leading Jewish figures to Albert as they go by: Pinhas Rutenberg, who obtained the concession for the electricity supply for Tel Aviv, Jaffa, Haifa, and all the major towns—except Jerusalem; Ehud Ben Yehuda, the son of Eliezer Ben Yehuda, the man who took the Hebrew from the Bible to make it into a modern language; and Zalman Shazar, editor of the *Davar*, the Labor Party's daily newspaper.

"The ideology, the promotion of Hebrew, troop morale . . . that's Zalman. The man he's talking to is David Remez, he runs the Histadrut trade union empire and the gigantic Solel Boneh public works company."

"And the young woman who's with them?"

"This is the first time I've seen her."

Her womanly form, even from a distance, draws Albert's attention. She is moving, talking, laughing. Her thick black hair bobs vivaciously on her shoulders as she nods her head. The beige dress she is wearing is as severe as that of a worker in her Sunday best, but the way she moves evokes a great sense of freedom. She seems decisive and fierce, yet gracious at the same time. Not a grain of worldliness or affectation inhabits this woman who is very much in the present moment.

Golda is watching Zalman Shazar. Behind his silver-rimmed glasses, her lover's eyes are constantly moving, as if they were absorbing reality at full tilt and registering every detail. He says to her in a low voice:

"The Arabs are courting the British, but they're wasting their time. They're lost. They don't have a clue where they are nor what they must do. The English smile at us, but even the way they like us is anti-Semitic. They promised us a homeland in Palestine, they maintain that this country is our natural home. But really it's in order to send their own Jews out here and get rid of them on the cheap."

Night is falling, the garden lamps are lit. The various groups mingle more readily. Albert would like to leave. Oussama wants to stay. A man in his forties comes up to them—a Palestinian in a light-colored suit, with a thin mustache, a golden tooth, and a signet ring on his finger:

"The hermit of the Pink House, at last! Among all those I administer, you must surely be the most invisible. Allow me: Hassan Choukry, mayor of Haifa."

Albert shakes his hand. Choukry is the last person he would have wanted to run into. This notable of Turkish origin, whose power has always been based on his connections, does not inspire friendship in Albert. The British dismissed him, and he has been spending his time trying to prove that he is more pro-British than the British themselves, going so far as to support their project for a Jewish homeland. The local elections that he has just won, with two Zionist Jewish candidates on his list, have opened the doors to City Hall.

"Congratulations on your victory in the local elections," says Oussama to rescue Albert, who cannot say a word.

"Your reputation is well-known, Mr. Oussama, but it is not easy to meet you either. I know all the members of your family individually. I can't claim that they like me very much—political rivalry is a normal thing—but what unites us is stronger than that which divides us. Are we not all Muslims? Do we not share the same language and culture? We all belong to the same world and we are trying, each in our own way, to deal with new situations. It is said that you are in a class on your own. I would really like to know how you deal with these situations yourself."

"Poorly, I must say. Very poorly."

"Why?"

"I've been living in Haifa for some time now. I thought I would be able to live there peacefully, away from all the political fuss. But it is becoming increasingly difficult."

"And why is that?"

"Because of the Communists! I don't wish to incriminate your Jewish friends, they surely know nothing about it. But I think a certain number of Russian Jewish immigrants pretend to be Zionists in order to come to Palestine, and then they take off their masks and raise the red flag. Do you hear me? The red flag!"

"Of course I hear you. You needn't shout!"

"And what do they have to say, those Bolsheviks who have set up shop in Haifa? They say that the Arab peasants must rebel against their feudal lords, against the effendis who exploit them, oppress them and suck their blood!"

"No need to get so worked up . . . "

"I'm getting worked up because it's a scandal! My family and yours may have their political differences. But, all the same, we do agree to preserve the social order as it stands, to fight the Bolsheviks, the anarchists, and everyone who is trying to turn our peasants against us. That's the least we can do!"

Albert turns to one side to try to restrain his irrepressible laughter. He sees that several members of the Husseini tribe are displaying signs of nervousness. Oussama is completely out of control now, and doing his best to attract attention. Hassan Choukry, the sweat pouring from his brow, is trying to calm him:

"The Haifa Communists are just a small minority. They won't do anything to disturb the calm of the town or your own peace and quiet. As the mayor, I give you my word."

"I'll make a note of it, Mr. Choukry, but there's something much more serious than that. For some time now, in front of my house, in my own street, in the center of town and on the vacant lots along the waterfront, there have been more and more vagabonds. I don't know where they've come from or what they want. But there they are, idle, day and night, watching the passersby with their criminal stares and brewing up who knows what sort of evil deed. Hooligans. Riffraff. They are frightening everyone. More and more of them every day! I don't understand what the local authorities are waiting for to drive them out of town."

"My dear Mr. Oussama, it's not that easy. You know as well as I do that the majority of those people are harmless peasants who have lost their work and their land . . . It's not impossible that a few delinquents eager for vengeance have found their way into their midst . . . But it's not a reason to . . . "

"And why have they lost their work and their land? Because the land was bought up by your Zionist friends. And now you've got these miserable wretches on your hands. What are you going to do with them? They also fall under your administration, as far as I know."

"Not at all. They are not from Haifa. They are peasants who came to look for work in town. But there is no work. Even the Jews can't find work anymore! For strictly humanitarian reasons, I can't tell them to leave just like that. That would be too dangerous. And anyway, where would they go? The situation is the same everywhere."

"So you are telling me you can't do anything," insists Oussama. "So it's going to go on."

Not knowing where to turn, Hassan Choukry sees David Remez coming toward them, with the young woman.

"David, you are heaven-sent," he says. "I'd like to introduce two of my friends: Oussama el-Husseini, Hadj Amin's nephew, and Albert Pharaon, owner of the Pharaon bank."

"How do you do."

"This is my friend David Remez," continues the mayor of Haifa. "You must have heard of him. And Miss, Mrs. . . . "

" . . . Golda Myerson."

She has just made her own introduction. The confidence in her voice, her gestures and her gaze confirm Albert's first impression. While he is holding her hand in his own, he feels her tremble slightly, a shadow passes over her face, and she seems for a split second to lose her poise. And then immediately regains her composure, but the young banker cannot forget what he saw so briefly: emotion beneath the tough outer shell, a certain frailty. In any case, she is looking him in the eye, making no attempt to deny it. And seeming more attractive to him than ever. Something in her is scrutinizing, searching, there is something naked and immodest which makes him understand she will go right to the end—whatever that end might be. He can think of no better way to formulate it. This woman in her thirties, with her sharp features, is questioning silently and persistently, as if the puzzle in her gaze has not yet been solved.

Golda takes a moment to still her beating heart. She thought she was meeting one man, a banker, and then suddenly she saw another, her friend Noam Pinsky, brought back from the dead. A Ukrainian Jew who was born in the same town as her, but it was in Milwaukee that they met. He was twenty-three and she was fourteen. He was handsome, and he was the first man she would have liked to give herself to. She had even decided to do so, but two or three weeks later, during a fishing excursion on the lake, he fell into the water and drowned. His death has frozen him in an image of eternal youth. And suddenly here he is again, in Jerusalem, wearing a stranger's features. The resemblance lasts only a few seconds, and when Golda looks at Albert again, she does not find it so striking, even wonders

whether there really is a resemblance. The two men have neither the same nose nor the same mouth, and their foreheads
are different. But the banker's way of moving, of holding his
head, a kind of fluidity, all these immaterial elements create a
fleeting precipitate which brings Pinsky back to life. She has
registered his name, Albert Pharaon; a good name. Judging
from his clothes and his manner, he must be European. The
first words he utters confirm this impression: his English is
perfect. But the slight accent and his exotic name seem to con-
tradict the image. She isn't sure. She looks at him and can't cat-
egorize him, the way she generally does with people. He's a
hybrid, something of a paradox, an eccentric of the kind which
only the Levant can produce. Albert Pharaon.

He seems unusually nervous. Golda notices that he finds it
difficult to move away from her. Pinsky was the same. He
would look at her with a dreamy air and think, She is still too
young—or at least that is what she has always assumed. The
banker seems pensive, too. He is not even listening to the question Remez has just asked.

"Excuse me," he says, collecting his wits, "I didn't hear what
you said."

"I was asking whether your bank belongs to an international group or whether it is local."

Albert notices that Oussama el-Husseini is smiling with an
amused air, leaving him to cope on his own.

"It's a family bank, Lebano-Palestinian," he replies.

"And what if I said to you, Let's work together: what would
you say?"

"Work in what way, Mr. Remez?"

"It's hard for me to explain in English . . . "

He turns to Golda and speaks to her in Yiddish. She translates word for word:

"The Solel Boneh public works company needs financing
and your bank must surely be interested in developing the

country. You could lend us money against a certain interest rate, or invest in specific projects."

Albert hardly understands what she is saying. He goes no further than the sound of her voice. It is low and caressing; she needs no encouragement to convey her hidden strength. Even when she has finished translating, Albert gets the impression that their exchange is still going on.

"It all depends on the type of project," interrupts Oussama, with no sense of timing. "I am the director of Barclays in Haifa. If it's an interesting affair, my bank could associate itself with Albert Pharaon's."

Remez is surprised. He never expected a member of the Husseini clan to make such an overture. Golda is slow in translating, so he resorts to his poor English to ask Oussama what type of shared project might be possible.

"I was just speaking with the mayor of Haifa," he replies. "There are increasing numbers of people without shelter in this town. Why not collaborate on a major program of mass housing in order to give them a roof over their heads? We could finance it together, and Solel Boneh would take care of the construction. You have the experience: you are building entire colonies!"

Remez greets his proposal with a moment of silence. Then he smiles maliciously:

"Dear Mr. Husseini, there's not much point in playing at this little game for too long. There is business, and then there is politics. I merely wanted to talk business with you. What do you think, Mr. Pharaon?"

"I will not lend you any money," says Albert in a calm and confident tone, "any more than I will sell you one single *dunom* of my land."

"Why not?" asks Golda briskly.

"Because I am, as a matter of principle, opposed to any company which aims to develop Jewish society alone in Palestine."

Golda and Albert stare at each other for a few seconds, as if they are playing at who will be the first to lower their gaze.

"Do you know," says Remez with a smile, "I hear the same arguments on our side, in the Zionist movement. Some people want the national homeland idea to continue developing as a strictly Jewish thing. That was, after all, our intention at the outset. Others believe, however, that we have to collaborate with the local population and even build a bi-national society with them. I won't hide from you the fact that those who favor this second inclination are very much in the minority. How can it be otherwise if men like you, who are open-minded and wealthy, close all the doors to any form of cooperation?"

"I'm not closing any doors," Albert replies. "From a certain point of view I'm even glad you are here in Palestine. But I would like to speak in a concrete fashion. I am ready to put a pound sterling on the table every time you put one, on the condition that it be in order to finance a development project which will benefit both Jews and Arabs."

"We must talk it over in a more appropriate time and place," says Remez. "Here is my card."

His gestures are smooth, his confidence is natural, he has no time to lose. He bows slightly and takes Golda by the arm. But he had not reckoned with the Husseini clan's black sheep:

"This idea of shared projects is excellent! I'm sure Barclays as such would be interested. After all, encouraging cooperation between Jews and Arabs is the very foundation of the British mandate in Palestine. Here is John Fillmore; let's ask him. John! You know Albert, I believe. Would you like to join us for a moment?"

John Fillmore comes up to them with two other Englishmen, one in civilian clothes and the other in uniform, and he introduces them right away: Sir Charles Montagu, from the High Commissioner's cabinet, and Raymond Cafferata, chief of police in Hebron. Oussama sums up in a few words what has just been said. Fillmore seems unconvinced:

"In theory, it's a good idea, but it presupposes a strong political will. We all know that in Palestine the problem is not just financial."

"In the name of the mandated authorities," says Sir Charles abruptly, "I can assure you that His Majesty's government does view this type of project favorably. I am a member of Lord Plumer's cabinet, and I can affirm that if the initiative were to go any further, the High Commissioner would do everything in his power to encourage it."

Montagu's intervention surprises Albert. His appearance and manner suggest that the man is a typical British official in post in an ordinary corner of the Empire. In theory, he should be maintaining the low profile of his administration. But he looks as if he is suffering personally from the situation in Palestine. Golda translates his words into Yiddish. Remez suddenly seems very concentrated. What began as a rather overly provocative conversation is turning into an almost official exchange. Exaggeratedly friendly, he replies through Golda:

"I am glad to meet you, Sir Montagu. I knew your uncle, Lord Edwin Montagu, back when he was His Majesty's Minister. You are the descendent of an old and noble Jewish family, and it is an honor for me to welcome you *among us*, in Eretz Israel."

"The pleasure is all mine," replies Montagu, icily. "I've just arrived here in Palestine, this country where so many communities have been intermingling for so long. What do you think of the proposition we've just heard?"

"I find it very attractive. But you will appreciate that I am not entitled to answer for myself. I suggest we confer separately with our own people, before we think of meeting again to discuss it."

Albert's gestures, the way he has of lowering his head and

raising it again, revive the ghost of Noam Pinsky. As Golda is walking away with Remez, she turns around several times. It is like some bad trick that the East is playing on her. To avoid betraying her emotional turmoil, she asks Remez about Charles Montagu.

"He's the nephew of a Jewish Englishman who is a ferocious enemy of Zionism," he replies. "At the time of the Balfour Declaration, Edwin Montagu was a member of the British Cabinet. He sent an outraged letter to his Prime Minister, Lloyd George, telling him that if Palestine were to become the Jewish national home, 'every anti-Semitic organization and newspaper would ask what right a Jew has to fill a post of responsibility within the British government.' The nephew is no better. But we were warnéd too late. There was nothing we could do to prevent his nomination. And now there he is."

"And?"

"And, nothing. This type of skirmish is fairly common—it's a social game. The discussion we just had will be of no consequence. Everyone knows it. It's amusing to cross swords like that, from time to time."

Oussama is pressing him to leave, and Albert no longer wants to. Golda Myerson has left him in a strange state of mind, slightly stunned. He can say only that she impressed him, and even disturbed him in a way—but it is not an unpleasant disturbance. He would like to understand, but is not sure that it is that important. His desire is abstract, absent-minded. Simply put, he does not want to leave a party where he senses the young woman's presence. She is out of his sight, but her image has stayed with him—her gestures, her smile, the way her dress swayed as she turned to leave. He has not been this intrigued since . . . when? How could such a solid woman act in such a quivering way, particularly with him? And yet she belongs to the Zionist camp. Between Remez's position and her own he could detect no difference. Their gestures, the movement of their bodies, the glances they exchange all emphasize their shared familiarity, from which the rest of the world is excluded. Albert has the impression that he has involuntarily touched upon the young woman's sensitive spot, the chink in her armor. He himself is shaken, ill at ease, nervous. The mild hubbub around him suits him perfectly. The mayor of Haifa has wandered off. Oussama is trying to get Charles Montagu to speak, and has come up against the diplomat's impermeable politeness. Raymond Cafferata, the police officer, is more forthcoming, but no one is listening to him. Albert takes it all in from afar.

" . . . until the day I understood that it was her skittishness which was intimidating me," Cafferata is saying. "As soon as she sees me, she steps back and turns away as if she wanted to hide. It's the first time I've ever had such a relation with a mare—but what a mare!"

"You have horses?" asks Albert, suddenly back on earth.

He looks at the British officer for the first time: a pleasant sort of fellow, something rural about him, the son of someone important, perhaps, and despite his impeccable uniform he does not seem very military.

"They're not mine, they belong to the brigade in Hebron," he replies, "fifteen policemen on foot and eighteen on horseback, they're all Arabs with the exception of one Jew. We have a stable there with twenty or so horses. Nothing remarkable about them, but I like horses so much that I look after them. I admit I don't have a great deal to do. In Hebron there are no other Britons, only me—except for two old missionary women. The situation is calm, and that allows me to spend my days in the saddle, making the rounds of the forty villages under my authority. Do you know much about horses?"

That's it, now Albert understands. It was not what the person Golda Myerson happened to be saying or thinking which troubled him, but her animal self standing there across from him. The way she moved, laughed, looked back as she walked away. He had encountered something in her, a secret, an improbable mixture of wild beast and wounded bird. She did not lower her eyes. He now realizes that the emotion he felt when looking at her was the same he felt when looking at . . .

"Horses are my passion," he replies, his eyes shining.

"Come and see mine! They're not thoroughbreds, but they are highly strung and charming. I'll show you the mare I was just talking about. And the region around Hebron seen on horseback is marvelous. If you like riding, I'll give you a tour."

"How kind of you."

"Hmm . . . I must admit I do feel rather lonely out there . . . You will be most welcome, Mr. Pharaon, anytime!"

Other people are talking, Albert is no longer sure where he is. Oussama has vanished, and night has fallen. There is too much noise, voices sound too loud. The wind has shifted, bringing a strong fragrance of broom. A few yards away, an orchestra has started playing. Albert realizes he is standing at the edge of the dance floor set up on the lawn. The little group he was part of has dispersed. Alone now, he searches for Oussama in the crowd but cannot see him anywhere. To get away from the music as much as to hunt for Oussama, he crosses the entire breadth of the lawn, going against the flow of guests heading slowly toward the dancing.

"Are you lost?"

He turns around. It is she. That piercing gaze, again—but this time with a spark of irony that he had not noticed before.

"Completely," he replies.

She laughs, a short, cheerful laugh, surprising in a woman who looks so serious. She does not laugh for long. They look at each other easily, openly. Golda's eyes are very blue, almost translucent, and she can fix her gaze for a long time without saying a word. The guests are almost all on the other side of the lawn now, in the aura of light and music. Albert and Golda stay where they are, motionless in the darkness. She speaks again, straightforward:

"It was a real emotional shock earlier when I saw you. You remind me of a friend, a man I knew in America. It's very disturbing, because the resemblance comes and goes, a sort of eclipse."

"Who is that man?"

"His name was Noam Pinsky. The same height as you, the same gestures . . . and now, the same smile. It's terrible."

"Did he die?"

"An accident. A long time ago."

"I am sorry."

"You are not Jewish, by any chance?"

"No, why?"

"I don't know. It's strange . . . If you like, I'll show you a photograph."

"With pleasure."

He could add that he noticed her too, before he even met her. But he says nothing. He feels incapable of seducing her. This silence suits him, there is comfort in the mystery of feeling so good with this stranger.

"Do you know what?" she asks. "I find it very difficult to keep reminding myself that you are an Arab!"

Albert smiles without speaking. Her eyes light up, a brief sparkle.

"Why did you say, earlier on, that you were pleased that the Jews have come to Palestine?"

"I said: from a certain point of view."

"And which is that?"

"The one I see you from. Here you are, beneath an English sky. A stranger, and terribly attractive. No one can really seriously believe you are going to cause a Jewish state to be born in Palestine. But your fiction will play a role that you cannot imagine. You will throw us into the modern world the way you throw a lobster into boiling water. Without meaning to, you will arouse—and perhaps even cause it to explode—the absolutely stifling traditional society to which I belong."

"You take me for some sort of Prince Charming?" she asks, incredulous.

"Your methods are slightly more brutal."

She shakes her head and smiles:

"What am I doing here? I am the victim of a resemblance."

"You don't look to me like a victim."

"Well, I'm glad, but that doesn't change anything. In reality, you are off limits."

"You're not allowed to associate with Arabs?"

"Absolutely not!" she replies, laughing. "Besides, you're not Arab."

Her own words echo strangely to her ears. She wanted to make a joke, and her words fall into a prolonged silence. Neither one of them steps back. And because they are silent again, their closeness is disturbing. She has tied her hair back since their earlier encounter, revealing her forehead and her entire face. Albert observes the determination he can read in her piercing gaze, her fine lips. No makeup, no artifice. "A Jewess," he thinks, without really knowing what the word evokes in his spirit. He senses only that this attractive young woman is not raising any barriers against him—or against anyone. As if she simply had no defensive tendencies, none of those withdrawal tactics generally meant to keep others at a distance. He could reach out his hand and touch her, and she would let him.

She suddenly takes a step backward, as if she were tearing herself away. Just at that very moment, a sharp explosion is heard. A bright halo illuminates the sky, then is followed by others. Fireworks! The fireworks for the King's birthday. They had completely forgotten. The rockets soar skyward in rapid succession. Together they watch the endlessly luminous night sky. Albert steals glances at Golda. She looks enraptured. With each luminous burst she gives out a small cry of delight. She raises her arms toward the sky, then holds herself back, he can see she is holding back.

"Let's meet again," he says, his voice slightly hoarse, as he touches her arm.

She turns around to face him, so close that he can see the light of the fireworks in her eyes.

"Where?" she asks.

"Wherever you like, outside British protection."

"I am busy every day from seven in the morning until midnight."

"At midnight, then."

She holds his gaze, without a trace of hesitation in her voice:

"At my place, then, in Tel Aviv, next Thursday. I'll show you the photos of Noam Pinsky."

8

THE MEETING - 1929

She recognizes their voices in the stairwell. She holds the door for them, feeling transparent. They move into the apartment, help themselves to drinks, go out onto the balcony, settle in the living room, and never cease from talking: on his way through the old town of Jerusalem, Ehud Ben Yehuda saw Arab workers filling a crack in the Wall. Remez maintains that these so-called repairs are actually a pretext for gaining rights over the building. Katznelson suggests drafting a letter of protest right away to the High Commissioner. Arlosoroff thinks the only solution would be to buy the Wall and all the surrounding houses. Ben Yehuda replies that that is pure fantasy. The American millionaire Nathan Strauss didn't even want to give the five thousand pounds needed to buy the only house for sale in the area, the Khalidi house.

It is too hot, and nightfall has brought no cooler evening air. Golda is surprised by her own silence. Debate is ordinarily a pleasure in itself, a way of gathering under the same tent to speculate, argue, and belong, an old Jewish tradition. In the Seder prayer, a man is excluded if he fails to say *we*. Golda knows better than anyone how to say it, but not this evening. In spite of her efforts, she cannot bring herself to see this story about the crack in the Wall as anything vital.

It is ten minutes to eleven. The children are sleeping at her sister Sheyna's, she wanted to be free this evening. She has worked all day, obstinately refuting the idea of the nocturnal meeting she gave to Albert Pharaon. Now she wonders what came over her, to invite him to her house. She does not know who this man is, or even what he looks like. If she were to meet him in the street she is not sure she would recognize him. Even his resemblance with Noam Pinsky seems to be some sort of trick. She can recall Noam's face perfectly: that is Noam, and no one else. She looks at the clock again: five minutes past eleven. She feels she is growing nervous. A warm wind has risen, billowing the curtains.

" . . . but with Jabotinsky, who just settled in Israel, Ben Gurion is going to be overwhelmed on the right. Any acts of moderation on our part will seem like cowardice . . . "

Zeev Jabotinsky, him again. Since he founded his own political group, everyone has been talking about no one else but this brilliant extreme right-wing orator. Golda heard him in public once; he was proclaiming that the Arabs' visceral opposition to the Zionist project was perfectly natural—and that the only way to get around it would be to constitute a Jewish majority in Palestine, weapons in hand. His discourse went straight to the heart of all those who were ready to do battle. But to the British he is appalling, and threatens to bring on a general confrontation that the Zionist movement is not ready for.

"One thing is clear," Remez is saying. "Jabotinsky is gaining influence. We seem like diplomats and he is like a warrior. We can't just ignore this crack in the Wall."

Golda wonders what would happen if Albert Pharaon suddenly showed up in the middle of this assembly. She shivers faintly at the idea. The hour goes by and no one moves. She is annoyed by her own impatience and powerlessness. It feels as if she is spoiling everything, her own pleasure to start with: why did she get herself into this situation? She didn't need to get involved in something like this. If she'd been thinking for even half a second she would have called Pharaon to cancel—but she hates going back. What can she say to the others to get them to leave? At a quarter to twelve, she gets to her feet. To her great surprise, they all do likewise, as if it were completely natural. They've drafted a letter, the Wall will be protected, they'll talk again in the morning. They hardly say goodbye. Golda is alone. This solitude, far from calming her, leaves her incomprehensibly agitated. She has no time to think. She goes into the bathroom, looks at herself in the mirror, starts to brush her hair, and stops again, exasperated. She goes back to the living room, empties an ashtray, picks up a few glasses . . . Her face is flushed. She is under no obligation to anyone. Someone has just knocked on the door.

She opens and it is Albert. She recognizes him right away. Just as he was when she left him in the royal gardens, just as he is. All his clothes seem to be made of the same light and caressing fabric. His hands are empty, except for his hat. So he has come. She looks at him with surprise and thinks, "He's a mensch." He has strength, substance, an aura, there is something sharp, a distraught nobility about him, of his very own . . . In his eyes there is a glint of unwitting sensuality, a promise of excess. Of course she knows him, she has not forgotten him. Not a great deal remains of his resemblance with Noam— unless it is, for her, this strong impression that he is someone familiar. A stranger who is not a stranger. Nothing seems more natural to her than to find him on her doorstep. His aristocratic mien goes well with the water meter and the yellowish roughcast of the stairwell.

Albert is astonished that the door has opened, and there she is. He has the absurd impression that he has caught her unawares, and this in itself surprises him. The wind and the sound of the waves enter with him through the front door. He looks at her, cannot stop looking at her. Here she is, this is where she lives, in this building in Tel Aviv overlooking the sea, behind a little metal plaque where he deciphered the name "Myerson" in Hebrew. All this time, she has been on his mind.

Golda Myerson. Her determined features, her open expression, her body, vulnerable. It really is her. He recognizes her from the physical sensation she arouses in him. Her black hair is tied back on her neck. She is wearing a white dress, because of the heat; it is light and flutters in the breeze. Her neckline is modest, her breasts strain against the cloth. Her skin is suntanned, a fresh, ripe fruit. There is something pained in her gaze, she is observing him closely, she is not afraid. Then, suddenly, she looks away. She is overcome. He has the impression he is intruding in her world, breaking a window at this very point in time, only to find her there across from him, distraught, caught in a moment of her life.

He comes in. She does not step aside. The door bangs gently in the wind. The quiet sound is like a signal: they are alone. They stand there motionless, unable to speak, so close that their faces become blurred. With her arm Golda makes a faint gesture of welcome which goes unnoticed. Nervously, she fiddles with a lock of hair, grows pale, it's unbearable, something is rising in her and is close to overflowing, he believes she might fall. He reaches out and holds her by the elbows. She looks astonished, steps closer. Albert's arms close around the small of her back. He does not kiss her, or embrace her; he says nothing. He inhales her scent, her cool breath, the turmoil inside her. With a deep sigh, scarcely audible, she leans against him. Just the contact of their two bodies. He sees the curtains swaying in the door to the balcony, the glasses cluttering the coffee table, the smoke-filled living room vibrant with echoes. He can sense the presence of men. Their warmth is still there, around her, Golda, the only woman in their midst.

He smiles to her, she gazes at him with a new gravity. Very slowly, she raises her hand to him. Her eyes are shining, but her gesture is that of a blind person. Her fingers trace the curve of his cheekbone, the hollow of his cheeks, the line of his jaw. They slip rapidly over his lips, meet on his forehead to slide down again, closing his eyes. In the same impulse she yields, all at once, like a dam breaking from the pressure. They are thrown against each other, they lose their footing, lose their self-control, no longer know what they are doing. Their bodies clash, tear at each other without restraint. Their parted lips seek, find each other. They do not have enough teeth to bite with, arms to embrace with. Every channel is open, every blow is allowed. They assault one another repeatedly; even their caresses are burning. In the midst of their kisses they draw back and contemplate each other with incredulous eyes, stunned that they recognize each other, still standing, still game. It is stronger than they are. Albert does not even realize when his broad palms slide beneath Golda's dress and run over the secret of her skin, tingling with pleasure. Her hands reach up to pull off his tie, she tugs at his white shirt and opens it with a sudden gesture. She leans over, her fingers curl into a fist, her lips devour, breathlessly, her lover's smooth chest. She pauses, he stops too. Suddenly very calm, they look at one another. They wait, for a long time, for their eyes to say yes.

"That's him, that's Noam Pinsky," murmurs Golda, pointing to the photograph.

"He doesn't look anything like me!"

"Yes, he does look like you."

"No one has ever taken me for a baseball player!"

She laughs. They are sitting on the stone floor on the balcony, a single sheet over their shoulders, the photo album on their knees. The wind is cooler, the air is almost pleasant. Through the railing of the balustrade, they can see the iridescent sea where the moon trails a large luminous ribbon from the horizon. Nothing is moving, not even the crests of the shimmering waves. Albert can scarcely believe that Tel Aviv's shoreline is actually Jaffa. But if he leans forward he can see the lights of the Arab town. Far from convincing him, the nearness of the town gives him the impression that he is viewing his own country from a foreign land. And he discovers with astonishment that this strangeness is pleasing to him.

"The photo was taken in Boris Schoenkerman's drugstore, in the heart of Milwaukee's Jewish quarter. Everyone would meet there to go shopping, do business, ask for advice. There were workers, lawyers, matchmakers, political militants, merchants . . . "

"Did they all dream of coming to Palestine?"

"Most of them were happy to be in Milwaukee and were doing all they could to integrate. There were only a few Zionists. Nobody took them seriously. Everyone thought they were dreamers who might compromise Jewish loyalty toward America."

"And you, what were you doing?"

"I was thirteen or fourteen years old and the others were at least eighteen. I was a Zionist, but too young! They would have nothing to do with me. So I went my own way. At the age of eleven I organized my first meeting and at twelve my first demonstration."

"And Noam Pinsky?"

"He would have nothing to do with me either! He said I was his little sister, but he grew dreamy around me. He wasn't even a Zionist. All he cared about was sports, physical exercise, his body. I was fascinated. But in his face there was something sensitive, vulnerable . . . It's true, he really did look like you."

Albert watches her in silence. She is sitting cross-legged, her knees touching his, her hair loose on her shoulders. She is in Milwaukee, on this Tel Aviv balcony, an adolescent with broad shoulders, her face held up to the future. What she has lived is as present within her as what she is living. She is completely at home in herself. There is no superfluousness, no margin for pretense. With the flow of her words, the stories she is evoking unfold across her face, it is moving, changing, taking on colors.

A magic lantern, thinks Albert. She inhabits all of time. Like a creature moving through darkness, trusting only its instinct. Just like an animal, whole, intuitive, sensual . . . He reaches forward and takes her gently by the arms.

She is startled, breaks off, smiles. She understands that he is no longer listening. Her shoulders have never rolled like this in a man's hands. He is staring at her, as if he wanted to say something to her. His mute intensity can find no means of expression, he seems upset, a fine film of moisture in his eyes. She senses that she has upset him, but why? His hands are holding her, firmly. She responds so eagerly, her head and arms and shoulders thrust forward, her fingers curling around his neck, her burning lips everywhere on his face. Sitting cross-legged, their position prevents their bodies from meeting. They press themselves up, arch their backs, rise up on their knees, pull at one another with all the strength in their arms, in vain. They hide in each other's neck, hold each other's shoulders, lie down on their backs, laughing uncontrollably. The sky has faded to pale blue. They are calmer now. Golda extricates herself and starts to get up, wrapping herself in the sheet, uncovering Albert's body as she does so. He sits up straight on the cold floor. His arms behind him, his face held skyward, he watches her with a smile. "Even naked, he is elegant," she thinks, in a rush of rapture.

"Come. We can't stay here."

He gets up and follows her.

He opens his eyes and for a few seconds wonders where he is. He does not know this room full of furniture, nor these walls where Zionist leaders stare down at him. It is like being in the Soviet Union. Golda is lying on her stomach in a tangle of sheets. He cannot see her face. This woman lying naked across the bed is as foreign to him as all the others. He can say it to himself, so he does. She is beautiful, seen from behind. Her amber-colored body emerges waist-high from the sheets, as if she were rising out of them. A robust young peasant girl's body, not at all stocky but slim and firm, with round bones drawing soft contours. Her loose hair covers half of her back, caught by her last movement. She is asleep. The window is open wide, and the light announces an imminent sunrise. The small alarm clock on the desk tells him it is five o'clock. Albert has only just noticed the presence of the desk. There is also a cupboard full of paper, shelves stacked with files, a dresser without a mirror, a cello in its case, children's toys. The space has been filled according to the principle that everything must fit, be put away after a fashion, with no other aesthetic considerations. But this spartan, efficient side expresses a vitality hardly lacking in strength.

He gets up without making a sound and goes to the window. The sun is directly opposite, poised on the horizon. Horizontal beams of sunlight take form, shining with the dust between the houses. The streets are deserted. This is a foreign city. Albert seeks out any detail which might situate the town in a geography. There are no mountains, only a flat landscape, and the sun behind him. From this window he has learned that the planet Mars has landed in his country, and he is on board. To his surprise, he is wishing himself a good trip.

When he turns around, he is struck by the anxious look in Golda's eyes. On her knees in the middle of the bed, she is holding the sheet against her chest as if she were breathless, as if the love she has just acknowledged were about to fall away or fly out the window. He gives her a broad, trusting smile. She remembers him from his smile, from the way he sways on his feet, walking toward her and spreading his arms. He watches every change in her, the way her fear becomes relief, and her face suddenly lights up, despite a lingering trace of sadness.

He holds her tight in his arms, their bodies come together, find each other. He has lost all sense of time. He knows only how difficult it has been to reach this place, how painful the pleasure. Without wanting to admit it, it has occurred to him that daylight is a threat. Surely she has also felt it, and this is what has made their lovemaking so fierce and desperate. He recalls it as if it were a dream, and can retain only fleeting images upon awakening.

She is wearing a lightweight dressing gown, pale blue, belted at the waist. She looks like a worker. Despite her efforts, her nervousness betrays her. She insists on making him a cup of tea, and something to eat. He does not know how to refuse. Separation is in their eyes, but they do not mention it. They sit next to each other at the wooden table, in the tiny kitchen, and make no pretext of speaking. They gaze at each other continuously, forgetting to lift their cups to their lips.

Then he is leaning against the door, leaving. He holds her in his arms, motionless. The day has almost completely risen, their faces are in darkness. Their noses touch, their eyes are drowning, they can't do it.

"Tomorrow?" murmurs Albert.

This single word causes a revolution. Golda blushes, becomes agitated, shakes her head, forces herself to quell her dismay:

"No . . . Not tomorrow, it's impossible. Tomorrow, I'm leaving on a trip for . . . five days. I won't be back before . . . next Wednesday. The children will be here. But Thursday . . . "

She seems very upset. Albert smiles again:

"Thursday, then?"

Her face lights up. She nods.

"Here, same time?"

She nods again, several times. Her distraught gaze, lighting up despite itself: Albert will take it with him, for a long time.

9

Hebron - 1929

Golda steps down from the train and heads quickly for the way out. She is met by a stifling heat on the station sidewalk, much more oppressive than the heat in the desert at Beersheba, where she has just been. There is no wind. The air, saturated with humidity, is like some damp obstacle one must penetrate. She clutches the handle of her suitcase, the house is a ten minute walk from here. It is Thursday, noon, she is twenty-four hours late, not much point in hurrying anymore—and yet she hurries.

There is no traffic. A dozen or so jobless men are leaning against the wall, the sole sign of human life under the sun. Golda pauses to cross the street. She counts five unfinished buildings, abandoned. Perhaps her stay in the desert has opened her eyes. She has the impression that Tel Aviv is a ghost town, that the considerable amount of energy that enabled her to leave behind the sand dunes has vanished into thin air. She shakes her head: it's a heat wave, it's August. People have deserted the city: the wealthiest among them are traveling, the British are on leave, and the Jewish leaders are at the Zionist congress in Zurich . . .

As she climbs the stairs she hears her door open and the patter of little feet rushing down the steps to meet her. *Ima! Ima!* Her children's cries resonate in the stairwell, in her heart. She puts down her suitcase and opens her arms. They hug her for a long time, between their laughter and their tears. Kneeling on the landing, she kisses them over and over before she is able to speak:

"I was supposed to come yesterday, I know . . . " From their radiant faces, she can see she has already been forgiven. "But I won't go to work today. We can stay together until this evening!".

Menahem and Sarah dance around her, exclaiming with joy. Their happiness brings tears to her eyes. The babysitter comes out and takes charge of her suitcase. Golda climbs the steps to her house, carrying her children on her hips.

She busies herself in the kitchen, preparing the midday meal, cookies, a cake. Menahem and Sarah have put little aprons around their waist. They cling to her, are underfoot, speak at the same time, give her news of Morris, with whom they spent their last Sabbath . . . She is in their room, tidying, mending, sewing, replacing missing buttons. They interrupt her constantly, to show her their drawings and make up for the lost time. Everything happens quickly, and slowly at the same time. With energy and gentleness, Golda acts as if her home were indeed a home—and as if she were an authentic Jewish mother.

She sets the table herself. She ties the napkin around each child's neck, serves them, watches as they eat. Her flesh, her blood. Menahem eats ravenously, looking at her with shining eyes. Sarah is smaller, and needs help. A knock at the door. Golda puts her fork down.

A young Arab is standing on the landing, tall, olive-skinned, thick-lipped. A flush of heat rises to Golda's cheeks, she thinks Albert has sent him. He opens his mouth, he is Jewish, he is speaking Hebrew. Recovering from her confusion, Golda asks him to repeat what he has just said.

"Ben Zvi wants to see you in Jerusalem. I've got a car waiting downstairs."

"What's going on? I'm not aware of anything, I just got back from the desert."

"There was a demonstration yesterday and things went wrong."

She brings him inside, closes the door. The children have stopped eating. Their forks in the air, their eyes open wide, they already understand.

Before he begins, the young man tells them that his name is Shlomo—but he didn't always use that name. He has an accent: he doesn't pronounce his "kha" or "ha" like other people do, and he says Yaafa instead of Yafo. He is too talkative, he can't stop himself. He was born in Damascus, where his father was a merchant, and he grew up among the Arabs, he knows them well, he asserts, you can't trust them, the only way is to conquer the country with weapons, you can't make them understand otherwise. His gaze is feverish, both excited and frightened at the same time. She interrupts him:

"What was the purpose of the demonstration?"

"For Abraham Mizrahi."

"Who is that?"

"A young seventeen-year-old Jew who was living in the Arab village of Lifta, not far from Jerusalem. He was playing soccer with his friends, and the ball landed in a tomato patch. He went to fetch it. But a little Arab girl had found the ball and was trying to hide it under her clothes. He wanted to take it from her, she began to scream. Her parents and other peasants came running, someone struck Mizrahi with an iron bar and split his skull. Word reached Jerusalem about his death. That same evening, an Arab was struck in the head with a club . . . but he didn't die."

"And?"

"Mizrahi's funeral yesterday turned into a demonstration. I was with those in charge of keeping order. We made human chains to try to stop people from getting near the Wall. Our leaders had said clearly: don't let things get out of hand. But it was impossible. Most of the demonstrators were from the Betar, Jabotinsky's youth movement. They had clubs and they went into the Arab neighborhoods and started beating passers-by, and a few of them had to go to hospital. Then they broke through all the lines and made it to the Wall. They pulled out the national flag and began to sing *Hatikva.* The British soldiers charged, quite violently, but each time they closed ranks again and shouted, 'The Wall is ours! The Wall is ours!' and waved their flags."

"And what were you doing?"

"If I wasn't supposed to be with the team of stewards, I'd have gone and joined them. At least it's clear what they're saying. And the Arabs are raving mad now."

The young man is driving through the deserted streets with a nervous yet sure hand, and she can tell he likes this. With his sunglasses and his short-sleeved khaki shirt, he's playing the hothead hero. But behind his mask of confidence, Golda senses something like fear. He may deny it, but the situation is dangerous, and his stomach is in knots.

"Our leaders wanted to hold a reconciliation meeting with them today," he continues. "At Charles Luke's place—he's filling in for the High Commissioner. Before going, Ben Zvi brought us all together to give us a warning. He insisted that the slogan, 'the Wall is ours,' was a criminal provocation. He was practically yelling at us: 'You know perfectly well that the two great mosques are above the Wall and that tomorrow is prayer day for the Muslims. Thousands of peasants will be coming from all over the region, and some of them will be armed. There is so much anger that things could go very, very wrong. So it means we have to calm things down, it's our only chance.' I've never seen Ben Zvi so worried. Everyone is in Zurich, he's all alone."

"I have to stop off at the main telephone office."

Golda realizes she will never be home before midnight. She waits a long time at the telephone office for her connection to Haifa—and when it finally goes through, the phone rings and rings with no answer. She is at an utter loss; the vision of Albert coming to her house and finding no one at home is unbearable to her. During her entire stay in Beersheba, she nourished the idea of her meeting with him. Now she no longer knows what to do. Shlomo is waiting for her outside, she goes to join him.

Jerusalem is not as hot as Tel Aviv, but it is every bit as deserted. The moment they enter the town, Golda senses that the silence is somehow different. Here it is an invisible tension that has emptied out the city. All the shops are closed. Not a single policeman, not a single soldier. As if the city were abandoned to itself. The inhabitants are behind their shutters, and there is something ominous about the empty streets. Shlomo drives close to the curb, his eyes peeled.

"In Tel Aviv, you all live together," he says, "you can end up believing that the Arabs don't exist."

The street doesn't belong to us, thinks Golda, rediscovering a familiar fear. Here, they are everywhere. The street signs, the shop fronts, even the very air speaks Arabic. All her senses are on alert. She is overcome by a strange exaltation. If this crisis has an odor, then this is it. Fleeting figures appear—Jews, Arabs? They glance at the car slowly driving by, a sidelong, last-minute glance. There is fear in their eyes.

At the Jerusalem telephone office, she finally gets through. With a voice that is hardly as firm as she would have liked, she asks to speak to M. Albert. The male voice at the other end of the line repeats, in English, "Not here!," unable to add anything else. Golda calls Shlomo over: "Don't give a name. Just say that the person Monsieur Albert was supposed to meet this evening won't be able to come. That's all." The young man takes the receiver and begins to speak in Arabic. He seems to be so at ease in this language! His words flow, he smiles, his face changes, becomes almost childlike. He holds the receiver away from his ear briefly and whispers in Hebrew, "He's Egyptian, he has an Egyptian accent . . . "

At the party headquarters on Yafo Street, a zombie opens the door to them. Ben Zvi, the tall, slender man whom Golda has always found full of confidence, seems to have collapsed inward upon himself. His complexion is gray, his gaze is sullen, he is absent with the effort of preserving his concentration. Conversations come to a halt as soon as he enters the room. The two other negotiators follow him, heads lowered. Without saying a word, the young militants Golda was waiting with form a circle.

"We tried everything," says Ben Zvi, "but we got nowhere: there's no agreement, and no joint statement."

He falls silent. Everyone is silent. Ben Zvi's gaze meets Golda's. She has known him for over ten years. The first time they met was in Milwaukee, when he came for a meeting with the other Ben, Ben Gurion. She found out that he was born in Poltava and grew up in the same countryside as she had. He was an intellectual, but a military man as well: in Russia he had devised a self-defense system against the pogroms, and then in Palestine, in the Jewish colonies, a network of armed guards. Now he is in charge of the Haganah, the nascent Jewish army. And this only makes his fear all the more worrying.

"The mufti's representative wanted us to sign a declaration recognizing full and complete Arab sovereignty over the Wall," he continues. "That's not what we were sent there to do; we were ready to sign a joint communiqué making a solemn appeal for calm. We talked for hours but couldn't find a way out of the stalemate. So Charles Luke suggested we at least make an announcement that we had met and talked, in the hopes of defusing some of the tension. But Jamal el-Husseini said no."

He seems to go off in a daydream, as if mulling over the ins and outs of the failed negotiations. The militants wait with bated breath for his next word. He continues:

"Finally, we agreed to schedule another meeting . . . but not until Monday. That means that tomorrow, Friday, everyone will be on his own."

"What can we do, and why are we waiting to do it?" says Golda, less out of a need for an answer than to ward off the growing despondency she senses around her.

Something in her tone of voice seems to reach Ben Zvi. He looks at her for a long time, then nods his head. A faint smile rises to his lips, restores a bit of color to his cheeks, at last he is there with them.

"The British won't be of much help. Charles Luke, who's the interim High Commissioner, is a Hungarian Jew, but he wants to appear British first and foremost. And he has neither the authority nor the means: for the entire country he has only fifteen hundred policemen, most of them Arabs, and one hundred and seventy-five British soldiers. He called Amman before my very eyes to ask for urgent reinforcements. But when will they get here? In fact, all we can really count on are our own forces: we have the night to prepare our self-defense."

Now that he has started, Ben Zvi goes on to make a list of the measures that must be taken: remove all available weapons from their caches, distribute them according to the established plan, watch out for the British, who are watching them, go over the different neighborhoods in Jerusalem and prioritize the ones where the Jewish residents are particularly isolated . . . Gradually, those in charge of the different law and order teams regain confidence and begin to organize their meager troops. As for Golda, she is asked to sit by a telephone and devote her night to alerting the Zionist movement worldwide—the principal leaders gathered in Zurich to start with.

"Unfortunately, Ben Gurion can't get here until Saturday," concludes Ben Zvi. "And the same thing for the High Commis-

sioner. Between now and then we'll have to hold out. If Jabotinsky's people don't pour too much oil on the fire, we have a
chance of limiting the damage in Jerusalem. The real problem
is Hebron: six hundred Jews live there in the middle of twenty
thousand Arabs. Ten days ago I offered to send some men to
protect them, but they're old-fashioned Jews. They replied that
they'd been settled in that town for over eight hundred years,
and that their good relations with their Arab neighbors was the
best protection. Hebron is half an hour's drive from here. If
anything happens, there is strictly nothing we can do."

Once they leave Jerusalem behind, the road becomes narrow and follows the contour of the rounded hills which lead to
Hebron. On either side, the fields are deserted beneath the
sun: Friday is a day of rest. It is early morning, but the air
which comes in through the windows brings no coolness.
Albert doesn't mind. The spicy odors and buzzing of insects
fill his senses, and immerse him in a dreamy state which is anything but unpleasant. He wonders again who the Syrian who
called yesterday might be. According to Najjar, he was from
Damascus—he could tell from his accent, very different from
that of Aleppo. That was all he could tell him. Did he hear a
woman's voice, was he sure of the message, was there any question that he should call back? Drawing his brows together,
Najjar scoured his memory one last time but could find nothing else. Albert spent his evening watching the telephone, then
went to bed late and woke up early. No news. Unable to overcome his disappointment, he could not sit still. This trip
through the scorched countryside, empty of human presence,
was exactly what he needed.

He stops his car in the yard of the Hebron barracks, content
to be back among the stables and the smell of horses. This is
the third time he has responded to the invitation police officer
Cafferata made to him in the king's gardens. Today his host is

already in the saddle, girthed in his khaki uniform and wearing his pith helmet. An Arab interpreter is translating his instructions to five or six policemen, also on horseback. As soon as he sees Albert he dismounts and walks over to him.

"I tried to ring you this morning," he says.

"Did you want to cancel?"

"I got a call from my superior officers asking me to inspect the villages. Nothing special. There was some trouble in Jerusalem. I'm instructed to make sure everything is calm. Since you're here, come with me. I'd already saddled Amir for you."

Albert had not spent much time exploring the region before going on these horseback rides. The religious climate in Jerusalem was unbearable enough, and Hebron did not seem to be much better, in his opinion. But in Cafferata's company, it was different. The police officer who suffers from solitude has made him feel at home around horses again.

With the Arab policemen following a few yards behind, the two men ride at a walk down the main street of Hebron. Cafferata tells Albert what he knows. There were clashes this morning outside the mosques overlooking the Wall, and a certain number of Arabs armed with sticks and knives headed for the Jewish quarter. Several people were injured.

"It's been festering like this for almost a year," he adds. "Two communities with knives drawn, ridiculous quarrels over the Wall, rumors that lead to explosions . . . Around the time of the Yom Kippur festival, the Jews put up a screen in front of the Wall to separate the women from the men. The Arabs saw it as a change in the status quo. To their eyes the screen was merely a first step that would lead to chairs, then benches, then little walls supposedly to protect the faithful from bad weather. In short, the screen had to come down right away. Unfortunately, the man charged with the mission was one Sergeant MacDuff, an overzealous British officer. He showed up with ten armed men in the middle of the faithful who were praying. It was like a battlefield. The *shamosh* clung to the screen and was dragged along the ground for several yards, and the screen was torn. The Jews shouted out that this was a sacrilege and organized a demonstration, the Arabs responded with other demonstrations. Ever since, it's been war. Day before yesterday, the very same MacDuff brutally repelled the Jewish demonstrators who were shouting, 'The Wall is ours.'"

"I thought the Wall already belonged to them, and had for a long time."

"So did I. But it would seem it doesn't. We'll never find the way out of this."

"Are you worried?"

Cafferata smiled broadly. "If Sergeant MacDuff minds his Ps and Qs, the disturbances in Jerusalem will fade away on their own. And in Hebron the situation is perfectly calm."

The two horsemen ride past the cave of Machpelah, reputed to be the tomb of Abraham, where the Arabs built the mosque of Ibrahim; its minarets now overlook the center of the town.

"It's half past twelve," says the officer, "and the Jews will be coming out of prayers. Two hours ago it was the Muslim faithful who were praying at exactly the same spot. Do you feel any unrest? The Jews of Hebron have gone through the Arab empire, the Ottoman Empire and now the British mandate without mishap. It is true that since the Balfour Declaration and the influx of Jewish immigrants, the Arab kids have been known to toss a few pebbles at them from time to time. But on the whole their relations have been based on trust. I can assure you it's not at all the same thing in Ireland!"

Cafferata's impression is confirmed when they stop to visit the mayor of the first Arab village, then the second, then the third. Wherever he goes, the representative of British law and order is well received. In living rooms ringed by low divans, the notables serve tea and perform all the rituals of hospitality. The harvest has been good, the barns are full, there is no rea- son to complain, God be praised. In village after village Caf- ferata ascertains that there are no serious grievances. There have been, to be sure, a few local disputes, but no one talks about the Jews or of any specific tension with them.

Nor is the climate any different among the Jews. Cafferata and Albert stop off at the hotel run by the Schniorson family: nothing to report. They visit the Talmudic school in the town, the Slovodka yeshiva, and find no one about except the *shamosh* and a young student bent over his books. They are then invited to the stone house belonging to the head of the community in Hebron, one Slonim, bank director and munic- ipal councilor, who assures them that all is well. All the same, the British officer decides to order the policemen accompany- ing him to stay behind and stand guard over the Jewish homes.

On their way back to the barracks, the two men are alone. They keep their horses at a walk. Albert is thinking about Golda. He sees her face, her smile, the determined set of her brow, her body lying against his. Ever since their missed appointment, his desire has been returning to him in cycles. He needs to see her and touch her; his relation to her defies any amorous category. He would like to ring Najjar, to see if she has called.

A group of horsemen is riding toward them in a cloud of dust. Pulling on the reins, Cafferata recognizes corporal Mohamed Beshara, whom he had posted to the northern entry to the town, followed by four policemen:

"The people coming home from prayer say that the Jews are cutting the throats of Arabs in Jerusalem!" shouts Beshara in his broken English. "One car after the other, they all say the same thing. I couldn't do anything, I had to let them through. They are all worked up, the news will spread through the town!"

Without a moment's hesitation, Cafferata orders the corporal to return to his barracks and call Jerusalem to ask for reinforcements and instructions. He demands that all the available men be sent immediately to protect the Jewish quarter. Turning his mount, he motions to the other policemen to follow him to the center of town. Albert does not stop to think, sets off at a gallop behind the others.

"So that is what you are asking, what you are demanding, Mrs. Myerson," says Charles Luke, white with rage. "And you, Mr. Ben Zvi! You want me to hand out rifles to the young Jews in Jerusalem so that these disturbances end in a pitched battle and Palestine slides into a civil war!"

"I'm simply asking that my people be protected," replies Golda, utterly furious. "All my people, including women and children! It's your responsibility, you represent the mandated power. And if you can't restore order, allow us at least to defend ourselves!"

"What you are asking will only make matters worse. And it is precisely because I am in charge that in response to your request I am giving you a categorical no!"

"We came through the Jaffa gate to get to your house," says Golda icily. "We met an old Jew there, utterly exhausted, covered in blood, who was trying to get away from his pursuers. He'd been standing by the door of his shop when a gang of hoodlums on their way back from the mosque went at him, beating him with their clubs. We asked one of our bodyguards to take him to hospital. I don't know to what degree you are seeking to forget your origins, Mr. Luke, or perhaps the Jews in Hungary were treated better than those in Russia or the Ukraine . . . "

"Please stop your insinuations at once, Mrs. Myerson! Do not forget that you are speaking to His Majesty's representative in Palestine!"

"A man remains a man, with or without His Majesty," Golda says. "During my childhood I also saw defenseless Jews covered in blood and running down the street not knowing where to go. And it is for that very reason that I came to Eretz Israel: to prevent such a thing ever happening again. I had no idea that the senseless hatred of Jews would follow us to this place. And that the representative of the British Crown would spread his arms helplessly and yet keep us from protecting ourselves!"

"Mr. Ben Zvi," replies Luke in a muted voice, "you are one of the principal leaders of the Zionist movement. In that capacity, I would ask you to tell your fellow Zionist that she has overstepped the bounds. You are not so naïve that you might believe that the situation of the Jews in Palestine is in any way comparable to what they experienced in central Europe. And in particular, you know very well that the hostility shown toward you by some of the Arab population is not altogether 'unfounded . . .'"

"What?" exclaims Golda. "Now you're finding excuses for the aggression we've been subject to? You, a Jew!"

Ben Zvi seizes Golda by the arm to stop her from talking.

"I represent the Zionist executive," he says in a toneless voice, "and you, Mr. Luke, the mandated authority. The situation is far too serious for us to allow ourselves to be blinded by passion. We'll draw our conclusions later on. For the moment, from one leader to another, I would simply like for you to tell me what you intend to do."

"Listen carefully. For the moment, there have been twelve people injured: nine Jews and three Arabs. No one has been killed, and it is certainly not the moment to be bringing out firearms. A detachment of British troops left Amman in the middle of the night. They should be arriving in Jerusalem at any moment. Until that time, the men I have at my disposal will do their best."

"But those men are overwhelmingly Arab!" cries Golda.

The telephone rings. Luke takes the call, listens for a few seconds, then hangs up:

"Two Arabs have just been killed in a stabbing in the Mea Shearim neighborhood. They are the first. This changes everything: from now on we can indeed fear the worst."

Filled with dismay, the two representatives of the Zionist movement leave the room. Ben Zvi turns to Golda:

"I am willing to swear that those two deaths are the work of Jabotinsky's youth movement. He wants to replace Ben Gurion by creating a climate of fire and bloodshed. This is terrible for the Jews in Jerusalem, and even worse for the ones in Hebron!"

The horses' hooves ring out as they gallop down Hebron's cobbled streets. In the first neighborhood, there are no signs of any disruption of the mid-afternoon siesta. The heat is crushing, and one deserted street leads to another. As they near the central bus station, the clamor and noise of a crowd can be heard. In a few minutes Cafferata has grasped that no one incited this crowd to gather. The several dozen people shoving their way onto the square had come spontaneously to take the bus to Jerusalem, in order to lend a hand to the Arabs who were "being aggressed by the Jews." Standing on a car, three or four men, including a sheik, are haranguing the crowd, who reply with shouts of "*Allahu Akbar!* God is great!" and, "With our life, with our blood, we will avenge you, our homeland!"

Wasting no time, Cafferata posts his men at the four corners of the square and, still on horseback, resolutely clears a path through the crowd. The arrival of British uniforms goes some way toward dampening the zeal of the orators and their audience. Cafferata rides up to the car which is serving as a podium, dismounts, and climbs onto the car. He stands next to the sheik, facing the crowd.

"Listen to me!" he cries, at the top of his lungs, "listen carefully!"

A wave of incomprehension goes over people's faces. The policeman-interpreter is not there. Turning to the sheik, Cafferata asks in low tones, "Do you speak English?"

The religious man shakes his head. Cafferata waves his arms in Albert's direction and a few moments later the banker is standing on the car next to him.

"It is true that there have been incidents in Jerusalem, but nothing very serious," shouts Albert, translating Cafferata's words. "No one is dead, no one has been killed! The news you've been hearing has been grossly exaggerated. There are two or three people with superficial wounds, but no one's life is in danger!"

"That's not true!" shouts a man in the first row. "I was in Jerusalem! I saw the blood, I saw the bodies on the ground!"

"I have just received the official report from my superiors," answers Cafferata. "It is true that in one street there were people lying on the ground to get away from the stones that were being thrown. But I'll say it again: no one has died! Jerusalem is completely calm now. Return to your homes!"

"Don't listen to that Englishman!" shouts someone in the crowd. "The English have always protected the Jews!"

"I heard our mufti, and he told us to take arms and go to defend our holy places," shouts the man in the first row.

Cafferata whispers to Albert:

"That's impossible. The mufti could not possibly have issued such a call in public. Ask that man to climb up here on the car."

Albert reaches out and helps the man to climb up. Cafferata scarcely leaves him the time to stand straight before asking, "Are you saying that you heard this yourself, personally, the mufti's call?"

"I heard that we have to fight the Jews until our last drop of blood," replies the man dully.

Cafferata and Albert are pale.

"From the mufti's own lips?" insists the officer. "With your own ears? I have a meeting myself, this evening, with Haj Amin el-Husseini. So, tell me the truth. Swear to me that you are telling the truth. Speak without fear. God is watching you and hears you."

The time it takes for Albert to translate slows down the rhythm. The crowd is listening, waiting intently for the reply which is slow to come:

"Uh . . . well it wasn't actually him," says the man reluctantly, "but a sheik who spoke just before."

"And afterwards," says Cafferata more loudly, "when the mufti spoke, what did he say?"

"He said we must remain vigilant."

"What else?"

"That we must keep calm."

A touch of color returns to the two men's faces.

"Did you hear?" shouts Cafferata, his words conveyed by Albert.

There is a movement of unrest and confusion in the crowd. The British officer immediately takes advantage of the hesitation:

"So you see! I was telling you the truth! Sizable reinforcements of police have left Amman and are on their way. They'll be in Jerusalem in less than an hour. The situation is under control. Don't listen to the extremists who are trying to set the two communities against each other. Don't fall in the trap, listen to your mufti! He is simply asking you to remain vigilant and to go home! Each of you go your way now, calmly!"

Cafferata raises his arm and motions to the four mounted policemen at each corner of the gathering. They move forward to divide the crowd, using the technique they were taught in police school. Confused by what they have just heard, the people comply. Shaking somewhat at the knees, Albert and Cafferata climb back in the saddle. Corporal Beshara appears on the far side of the square, his face bright red, his horse's flanks covered in foam. He spurs him on and forces his way through the scattering crowd:

"Captain, sir, hoodlums from all over the region are heading for Hebron, packed into any car or truck they can find! They're not even hiding their weapons. I saw them with my own eyes, heading in small groups for the Jewish quarter. They're going down the street in gangs. I don't know what could possibly stop them now."

10

Desire to Kill - 1929

Two whole days have gone by, and still no news. She doesn't have a telephone. She is the one who has to call and she hasn't called. He sent her a telegram, and then another one. Everything is repugnant to him. The Pink House has become a mere abstraction, as has the Bay of Haifa. He is nowhere. She isn't calling. The late afternoon heat creates moving shapes in the air. Najjar has changed into a white shadow. Barefoot in his jellaba, he serves the coffee, disappears, reappears, brings the evening papers dark with headlines. After Hebron, there was another massacre in Safad, assassinations in Jerusalem, Jewish colonies have been devastated all over the country, Arabs armed with clubs have been trying to get into Tel Aviv, violence reigns all over Palestine.

In revenge, Jews lynched several Arabs in Jerusalem. Frenzied young men went into a mosque and performed a ritual burning of the Koran. The High Commissioner returned from London in great haste and ordered the air force to bomb Arab villages in order to quash the rebellion. The answer he received was that the country was calm. The murderous madness vanished as quickly as it had come, leaving the two communities in a daze. Nothing more has happened, it says as much in the newspaper. The massacre was just a single instance of bloodletting, a parenthesis. Albert feels as if he is stifling, gets to his feet, picks up his keys and leaves the house.

It is only seven o'clock in the evening but the road along the coast is practically deserted. The waves are high, the swell coming from deep in the sea, almost black. Albert overtakes a few cars and British police vehicles out on patrol. He is driving fast. He reaches Tel Aviv in less than an hour.

At the edge of town, young men are checking papers and asking drivers to open the trunk. They look nervous; some are armed with clubs. Their gestures are authoritarian, their tone is curt. They show no consideration in the way they search the small trucks and Arab cars. This is the first time that Albert has come up against the Jewish self-defense militia. He doesn't have his papers, he never keeps papers on his person, it is inconceivable to him that anyone might ask him for his papers. He can tell already what is going to happen, and is mad with rage. The truck just ahead of him starts up, spewing out a cloud of black smoke. Albert shifts gears and moves forward a few yards. The militiaman's hesitation lasts only a second: he waves him through. No doubt he took Albert for a Jew.

Tel Aviv is transformed, a dead city. Albert does not feel the tension that preceded the catastrophe. Because the catastrophe has already happened. The city of cafés and night-life is visibly in mourning. Everything is closed. A few passersby scurry along the street. Militia keep a somber watch at the intersections. One last turn and he is there, in her street. His heart is heavy, his heart is beating, he drives past apartment buildings which all look alike, and he does not look up. Golda's is at the end. There are lights on every floor, except hers.

He turns off the motor, there is silence everywhere. The sound of the sea fills his ears and he wonders why he did not notice it before. It is not the calming ebb and flow of the waves but a continual rumbling, part of the air itself. Now the sound has grown deafening. Albert steps out of the car, slams the door and, leaning into the wind, heads for the entrance of the building. He sees himself climbing the stairs like a sleepwalker. Climbing, reaching the third floor: *Myerson* is still on the door. He feels strangely reassured. He looks down at his feet.

There are no letters sticking out from under the door, no telegrams. She is there, she is collecting her mail. He stands rooted on the landing. She is in Tel Aviv and she isn't calling him. Albert stares at the door and sees what is behind it, the living room, the low table, the curtains, the balcony, the vanished world.

It is almost midnight when he leaves his car by the wall around the Pink House. He took his time driving back. Najjar's white figure is waiting for him at the gate. Albert walks by without a word. His step is unsteady on the gravel. The moon has risen above the overgrown garden, coloring the sky with a deep, electric blue. He stops, his feet in the grass. The telephone is ringing. Before he has time to grasp what it means, he sets off at a run.

"It's me."

She says nothing else, he recognizes her voice. Deep, hoarse, only two syllables. He is mute, as is she. It seems to take an almost superhuman effort for both of them to speak. Then she says:

"You came to my door this evening."

No music in her voice, no softness.

"I was afraid for you," he says dully. "I have to see you."

"That is why I'm calling you," she continues, detaching her syllables. "You mustn't come anymore. That's it. And stop sending me telegrams."

Albert is chilled to the bone. He might have been offended, but he feels only an infinite pain. The silence on the line has changed, bringing emptiness where once there was fullness. Golda's voice becomes hoarse:

"With all that's going on, it's become impossible. And even if nothing were going on."

"Golda, listen to me. I was in Hebron. I saw it all."

She says nothing. She is taking her time to let his words sink in. And when she speaks again, it is as if she has been roused from a faint.

"Come, right away."

No sooner has she opened the door than she walks to the center of the room. The apartment is perfectly tidy, as if she no longer lived there. Standing straight in her faded dress, her body rigid with fatigue and tension, her face burning, she turns to face him. She remembers him, she remembers everything, but from a great distance. She is defensive, prickly: eyes of steel, an impenetrable armor. He recognizes an inner fire in her not unlike his own, and a similar inability to express what is inside. The desire to take her in his arms and feel her causes him to ache to his very bones. She turns away again. In the middle of this icy décor he tells her, in a low voice, what he saw in Hebron, the exhausted calm of the villages, the crushing sunlight, the harvests sleeping in the barns. Her jaw clenched, Golda is listening with her entire being. They face each other. Without once taking his eyes from her, he tells her how the rumor entered the town and spread, never meeting any resistance. It is too calm, too hot, people mass together, their blood begins to boil. Albert sensed the moment when everything shifted, when the crowd began to understand that everything that was forbidden—murder, rape, pillage—would, for an instant, become possible. He talks about the windows smashed onto the road, the neighing of frightened horses, the rabbi and his daughter running through the streets, the dark exaltation of the murderers who discovered that suddenly, between themselves and their victims, there were no more obstacles.

Golda feels dizzy. She would like a moment of silence, but Albert can't stop. Cafferata and eight policemen on horseback rushed to the Jewish quarter. They dispersed the rioters who were surrounding the houses and throwing stones. The Jews had taken refuge on the roofs. Cafferata called to them to come down and go home and lock their doors. Just in front of the Talmudic school a student's body was found, that of Shumuel Halevy, riddled with stab wounds. The *shamosh* had managed to save his skin by hiding in the well.

"All that time you were before my eyes," he says, lowering his brow. "I couldn't leave."

She doesn't react. Her body is so stiff that she hardly notices she is trembling. She is staring at a point beyond Albert, but still hangs on his every word. He has to speak. Cafferata begged relentlessly for the reinforcements that all his superiors refused to send. The night went by without incident, miraculously, and in the morning it seemed it was all over. As soon as the sun rose they set off again to patrol the streets. The Jewish shop owners were wondering whether to open for business. Schniorson the innkeeper came out of his pension with sheik Maraka; he had taken him by the arm, they were friends. The night before, they had repelled a gang of young Arabs who were trying to get at the Jews. Albert grows distracted, loses the thread. His story trails off.

"And then?" cries Golda.

"There were eighteen policemen on horseback. Cafferata, for the first time, gave them rifles."

He stops again. Golda's eyes are burning. He meets her gaze, and holds it:

"We heard shouts, people running, the noise came from a nearby street, we hurried over there, the last murderers were escaping, they'd come from Eliezer Dan's house, I'd met him once, now he was lying in his living room with his wife, in the middle of the corpses, fifteen of them, men, women and children, scattered in every room. In another house we found nineteen students, assassinated."

There is terror in Golda's eyes, a bottomless well, an ancient, mortal wound, brought back to the present. Albert knows that. She was four years old when she understood what a pogrom was. Her memory has left her with fear in her bones. The feeling has never left her. She was only delivered from it when she arrived here, in Palestine—*when she came home.*

She speaks gently now, she is truly speaking to him. She looks at him and sees him. Her face is very white in the half-light, her features grave. For the first time she lets herself slip toward Albert, and begins to accept him as a mirror. A very fragile beginning. And for the first time he no longer feels alone; perhaps she does not, either.

"I've been living in Palestine for nine years," she says, almost dreamily, "and I now realize how peaceful those years have been. I really believed that we would be free of such insane displays of violence. But the pogrom has followed us. The same drive toward death, the same blind hatred, the same smell of blood. The only thing that has changed, in the end, is the color of the uniforms."

"You can't say that," murmurs Albert, drawing closer. "There were Arabs lying in the street who were killed because they wanted to stop the rioters from going after the Jews. The lack of foresight on the part of the British has been criminal. If they'd had ten soldiers there, they could have prevented the tragedy. But Cafferata conducted himself with honor and courage. In one street, he ordered his men to cover two young Jews who were running away from the hooligans. One of them was hit in the head with a stone, the other was stabbed right in front of Cafferata's horse; the horse reared up and threw him. He got back up, took a rifle and another horse and went after the murderers. I heard him order his men to shoot into the crowd. He himself opened fire, killing one of the rioters and wounding three others. He was running everywhere, it was pathetic how alone he was. In Russia the authorities turn and look elsewhere when Jews are being killed. They let the rabble get on with it, if they don't lend a hand themselves. In Hebron, sixty-seven Jews were killed, but close to four hundred were hidden by their Arab neighbors. There was only a handful of murderers. This wasn't a pogrom."

A terrible icy rage, so strong it is frightening, transforms the young woman into a pillar of salt:

"Sixty-seven! Sixty-seven! How can you allow yourself to count them? And how many does it take to make a pogrom, in your opinion?"

"It wasn't a pogrom, Golda."

She is shaking from head to foot. Her eyes ablaze, an expression of intense hatred distorts her face, her fury makes her reel:

"All the dead were buried in a common grave; all the survivors were evacuated on the spot; there is not a single Jew left in a town where they had been living for eight hundred years. What do you call that, then?"

She is shouting. Albert understands that he must calm her down right away, and one word could change everything. But he cannot say the word. He is not even sure that he wants to. It wasn't a pogrom. He can hear her agitated intake of breath, as if she were getting ready to explode yet again.

"You don't know Palestinian society," he murmurs. "People are poor, three-quarters of them cannot read or write. They don't understand what is going on. Their land has been bought . . . their peasants have changed into ghosts haunting the streets of Haifa and elsewhere. They don't even know who to turn to or who to blame. For ten years the Palestinians trusted their leaders without realizing that those leaders were either powerless or were collaborating. And when finally they understood, some of them went berserk because they realized they've been victims of a senseless outrage. It's horrible. But you live in this land, among these people. You have no choice. You have to live with us."

She hasn't heard a thing, she is blind. But at Albert's last words she shudders, as if she'd received an electric shock. She would like to kill him, he can see that she would like to kill him.

"Us? Who do you mean by us? We came here so we wouldn't have to depend on anyone, do you hear? There's no other us! We arc 'us!'"

Albert hears her words like a slap in the face. His body stays where it is, as rooted as a mountain, absolutely refusing to move. It's not a decision, but proof. He cannot accept. His entire life is at stake, in this moment; her life too. She is standing there, shaking with rage, her face utterly distraught. But in shouting she has let off some steam, she can't go any higher. He walks toward her without knowing what he is doing. Fascinated, she watches him approach, watches as he seizes her wrists with the determination of a man who is taking what he is owed: this love. She struggles in vain. He holds her firmly by her shoulders and her waist, holds her against him to oblige her to look at him and recognize his face once again. She doesn't yield. Gathering all her strength she pushes him away with her arms and her hips, punching him, scratching him, shouting to the sky. But each of her gestures has a double meaning, each one leads her that little bit further back into the intimate space she shares with her lover. Some weakness for him subsists deep in her body, and he has never stopped sensing that. And when finally he responds and pushes her back, lashes out at her, they both accept the struggle. They will fight and tear each other apart. With their bodies they will struggle to the death, a bitter, merciless struggle, and there is nothing, at any time, that can assuage them. They are in a pitched battle, shoving, clutching helplessly at each other, overwhelmed by an irresistible desire to tear themselves to pieces, until nothing remains of this man and this woman and their impossible affair.

11

BEHIND CLOSED DOORS - 1929-1933

The summer has only just ended, and a first torrential downpour, still warm, announces the winter. There is no autumn in this country. The rain rouses Albert from sleep. The window is open, the wind rushes in, he finds he is alone in the room. Five in the morning. The walls are watching him. Golda's place is still warm, he can hear the water running in the bathroom. She comes back. Through half-closed eyes he watches as she walks across the space to close the window. Her hair is disheveled, sleep still inhabits her movements. Unaware that her lover is awake, with a shrug of her shoulders she lets her dressing gown slip and she is naked. Her body is amber, slender and round at the same time, ripe with vitality. She bends her knees and slips beneath the thin sheet. Albert closes his eyes again. In the darkness he can feel Golda's body drawing closer to his. He is lying on his back. She puts her arm around his shoulder, lays her leg gently across his thighs, wedges her hip against his. From the regular sound of her breathing he can tell she has fallen asleep again. A delicious warmth spreads across Albert's stomach, an unbelievable well-being. Their bodies, joined together, are weightless, and they are adrift on a flying carpet, unconscious.

Two commissions—one British, and the other mandated by the League of Nations—are traveling through the country to investigate the massacre in Hebron. Albert has testified before both of them. He hasn't told Golda about it. They have given up talking about politics together. They meet whenever they can, at night, in secret, and ask no questions. They have abandoned all words. Their sensuality is all the more wild, and mute, and hardly bearable, for this silence. Their mutual attraction is like an illness. Week after week, they have embraced and repelled each other in one and the same gesture, feeling wounded, inflamed, then starting all over again. *There is no one but us.*

From the balcony, wrapped in heavy blankets, they contemplate the last winter storm. Lightning illuminates from within the gray magma which blends sky with sea, monstrous waves crash against the coastal road, the damp sinks into their bones. Golda squeezes her lover's hands and is startled by each clap of thunder. Nature unleashed delights her, frightens her.

She talks about Kiev, where she was born. There was no sea there, a landlocked region. The first time she saw the sea was in America, and she felt her heart open. In Tel Aviv it is something else again. Golda believes that people who live in a town by the sea benefit from having this permanent geographical landmark. They know better where they are in space, and are more balanced. Albert replies that the sea has never been known to prevent madness. He suggests they go down to the beach there and then. She looks at him as if he has lost his mind. He tells her the only thing they risk is getting wet, she won't meet a soul, there's no reason to be afraid, the weather is so bad that even the Zionist leaders are staying home. Golda looks from Albert to the wild sea, several times. Her eyes are shining but she shakes her head. The mere idea of appearing with her lover in a public place fills her with panic.

Albert insists. They have never gone for a walk together, have never kissed outdoors. Laughing, he calls her a coward, a woman without courage. She pulls her blanket tighter. He grabs her wrist and makes as if to drag her toward the door. She resists, clings to the railing. She is laughing now too. The rain beats on her face, her blanket slips. Suddenly moved, Albert opens his own blanket and closes it over her nakedness.

They embrace, make love, the roar of the storm hides their cries and their shouts of laughter. For Albert, there is nothing extraordinary in and of itself about having a Jewish mistress. Haifa is full of stories of love and sex between Jews and Arabs; some even live together. It is Golda who is extraordinary. Her Zionism is a calling, a passion, the very salt of her life. She came to Palestine for that very reason, to be a Jew among Jews. If he were discovered, her Palestinian lover would cause the very principle of her political commitment to be blown to pieces. And since their affair cannot exist, it does not exist. Each time Albert visits it is by accident, a madness to which Golda succumbs on a regular basis. Her lover is an exception, a man without society, without a past, always naked. He could easily have rented or bought a house for her in an unfamiliar neighborhood, in Jaffa for example, on the outskirts of Tel Aviv. But that would have meant providing an anchor to an affair that Golda stubbornly denies. Everything must happen at her house, furtive moments, stolen moments, encounters which should have no future but which are constantly renewed. Albert can speak to no one of this love, except Nina, each time he passes through Cairo. Cut off from her family, an unhappy recluse, his favorite niece has become his only confidant, month after month.

One night when they are together a knock comes at the door. She does not panic, but gets up, slips on a dress and leaves the bedroom. Albert hears her turning the key in the lock to the bedroom. It makes him laugh. He has become the lover locked in a cupboard, and not just any cupboard, the one belonging to the saint of Zionist saints. It seems like the irony of history. He is waiting. No, he's not even waiting; he is there, irrefutable. He listens behind the door and can make out several male voices, speaking in low tones. Golda he cannot hear. He imagines her, sitting solemnly, naked beneath her dress. The door to the balcony is wide open, it is still summer. A short while later she comes back, and says nothing. She gets undressed, lies back down, turns over, sits up, lights a cigarette. For a long time she stares into space, exhaling the smoke through her nostrils with a sigh. She is miles away, he can hear her thinking. She shakes her head, lowers her forehead, lets her eyes come to rest on him. He sees that she is stunned to find him lying there next to her. He sits up. She makes as if to come back to him, interrupts him, recoils. The news she has just had makes her tremble with rage, she can't hold it in any longer. The British government has published a white paper reproducing the findings of the two commissions on the investigation into the events at Hebron. It has concluded that Jewish immigration is the primary cause of Arab hostility and of the slaughter, and therefore it must be brought to a complete halt in order to avoid any further massacres. Tears of rage fill her eyes. She takes hold of herself, withdraws, her jaw clenched on her unfailing indignation, spite, and determination. She is trembling. Albert no longer dares touch her. As he sits cross-legged among the tangle of sheets his motionless body strains toward her, his eyes open, his hands open to her. But inside he is overcome by a tremendous sense of relief. The immigration will stop. It is the end of the nightmare for the Arabs, and for the Jews the end of a disastrous utopia. Despite all the disillusionment—and even because of it—the protagonists will have to come back to earth, look at one another, speak to one another, recognize each other at last.

It is autumn again, he misses her terribly. A Zionist delegation is traveling through Europe to lead the campaign against the white paper, and Golda is a member. Albert follows her journey in the *Palestine Post* and other Jewish newspapers. He has even started learning Hebrew. In Great Britain, Golda addressed gatherings of women, workers, intellectuals and even Scottish miners. To this last group she explained that Eretz Israel and Scotland were the same size and shared the same status as an oppressed nation. The next morning she spoke in London to the convention of trade unions of the British Empire. Spurred on by the Arab, African and Asian delegates, the over-excited crowd would not let Ben Gurion speak. Pale, he withdrew. Golda rushed to the podium. Taking advantage of a moment of confusion, she shouted that the "right of return" of the Jews to their ancestral homeland had been guaranteed by the Balfour declaration and that now, thirteen years later, the British Empire was shamefully preparing to back down on its promises. She barely had time to say that the "pogrom against innocent Jews" in Hebron, as elsewhere, was a tragic illustration of the necessity for a Jewish national homeland before the Arab delegates, suddenly roused, began to make an uproar. "I trembled on hearing her courageous words," writes Ben Gurion in the newspaper. "Her speech deeply affected the conference. She spoke with genius and confidence, and bitterly, with pain and sensitivity." Golda is becoming the rising star of the Zionist movement in Palestine.

Albert almost feels proud of her. Her ability to throw all her strength into a battle that is lost from the start amazes him. She is made of flesh and blood, she struggles and suffers for real, but within the framework of a chimerical representation of the world. With its towns and villages and everything which forms the basis of its ancestral roots, Palestinian society is concrete and real in an utterly different way, as permanent and ancient as the cries of the peasants calling to each other from one terrace to the next. In thirteen years the Jews have acquired only four per cent of the land. They are the only ones who actually believe they have a chance of replacing one country with another. Albert may well be the hidden lover, but the reality in which they live, the two of them, is unquestionably his own.

She told him on the telephone that if he could come she would delay her return for twenty-four hours. He scarcely recognized her voice—full of laughter, impatient, excited. He took the first plane. The taxi is struggling along the winding uphill road, climbing ever higher. Each bend in the road opens onto an unbelievable panorama. The afternoon is drawing to a close, the angled light reveals wild flowers as far as the eye can see. The encroaching shadow only emphasizes the power of the reds and golds. Albert feels as if he is in the Lebanese mountains, except that everyone is speaking Greek. The landscape, the scents, the sensations are the same, with the advantage of this being a foreign country. In Cyprus no one knows them. In the car heading up to Kakopetria, Albert is as moved as on the day of his first assignation with a woman.

She is sitting at a round table on the terrace of the hotel. Her dress is white, and she is lifting a glass to her lips; the parasols have not yet been closed. Far behind her, two or three tables are occupied. Spring has come early, the season has not yet begun, there is almost no one. She sees Albert and gets to her feet, nervous; she refrains from running to meet him. Her face is radiant, and with surprise he notices that she is wearing make-up. Of all people! He draws closer, stops. They face each other, surrounded by other people; this has never happened before. They have nothing in their hands, only their desire. The moment lasts, a twinge in the heart, delight, dizziness, there is no need to hurry. They take their last step with a same sudden rush: everything they have not experienced before now, everything they have waited for, for years, now compels them into each other's arms. They embrace violently, amazed to rediscover the familiarity of their gestures and their bodies. The sense that they are breaking a taboo brings a catch to their throats. They look at each other, trembling. Neither one steps back. They are kissing under the open sky, for all to see.

The luxurious hotel, situated on the mountainside, seems deserted: they have it to themselves. They dine with champagne on the terrace, they drink and break their glasses. They walk through the village with their arms around each other's waist; the most ordinary gestures of love seem like marvels. Their desire sends them back to the hotel. Petals are scattered across the bed, the windows are wide open. Albert observes Golda's transformation, her newfound freedom. All night long, she vibrates with incredible jubilation. She clings to his neck. There is a celebration in her belly, in her eyes, in the languid, inventive gestures of her hands. Until morning her long hair streams across her lover's chest.

The night passes. With a heavy heart they take the same airplane and part on arrival. Only on arriving in Haifa does Albert discover why Golda was so joyful: the white paper has been rescinded. Ben Gurion and Weizmann succeeded in a scarcely believable tour de force: that of making the British Empire back down on a decision.

12

THE SEPARATION - 1933

Albert is headed back to the Pink House after a short trip to Beirut. The magnificent sunset over the Bay of Haifa does nothing to calm his soul. In the bathroom mirror he discovers his first white hairs. The Lebanese who own land in Palestine are selling it off, one after the other, signing papers as if the transactions were imaginary. For them Beirut is Paris, they think they have become French. And since Palestine is British, it belongs to another continent.

Najjar appears with a glass of lemonade. Albert hadn't asked him for anything. He supposes that the young servant is trying to show him a bit of warmth: his master's bad temper always causes him to panic. He puts the tray down and leaves again; Albert has not unclenched his teeth.

He has discovered that Zeev Jabotinsky is a regular visitor to the Lebanese capital. He likes it so much that he has rented a room by the year at the Hôtel Saint-Georges. One of Albert's cousins has described him as a witty and cultured man—not at all the fascist Jew you might imagine. He is invited everywhere. The important families are fighting over him, he has become a part of the landscape. And yet his discourse, for all that, has not changed: "hostility between Jews and Arabs is a natural thing, we must prepare for war." But he delivers it with such charm that the inhabitants of Beirut find it titillating.

Rumors about Albert's clandestine love affair with Golda have begun to circulate. Albert thinks that Irene is the one who started them. She has been living alone for several years, and has numerous lovers, but she likes the idea of telling people that her husband is sleeping with the enemy. Albert's two children look at him coldly. They've never really known him, and now they don't know him at all. The rest of the family are annoyed. Uncles, aunts and cousins are all afraid that Albert will be accused of working with the Zionists. Has he sold land to them, compromised himself in some way with them, are the Arab nationalists threatening to bump him off? It is not really that they worry about his life. They are just afraid that his purported relationship with Golda will be bad for business, harm the bank or their reputation. The Lebanese bourgeoisie welcomes Jabotinsky in their salons, but worries about Albert's clandestine Jewish love affair. That's Beirut for you!

Unfolding his legs, Albert bangs his knee against the coffee table. The glass of lemonade falls and breaks. Najjar comes running, he must have been watching behind the door. Exasperated, Albert gets up, goes inside, heads for his room, goes round in circles, returns to the garden. The young servant has just finished picking up the pieces. With broom and dustpan in his hand, he beams his finest smile to his master. Suddenly Albert understands why he is annoyed. Golda is sailing for New York tomorrow. She is coming tonight to Haifa for a concert, her last night, in his town, in the very heart of his world, and she has asked him not to go. He has agreed. He realizes how very violent this actually is: she has made him an accomplice in his own disappearance.

In the light of the beams, a large crowd is pushing against the gate beneath the electric lamps which spell out in giant letters "Azizé Beach." It is a free-for-all. In a cloud of dust a bevy of young boys, some of them shirtless, are shouting and shoving and trying with all their might to force an opening. Shlomo slows down, drives past them and continues along the surrounding wall up to the gate marked "Stage Entrance." He lets

Golda and Morris off there. Golda immediately recognizes the smiling young man on the poster. His neatly parted hair, his white jacket and bow tie, clarinet lying across his knees. His name, Benny Goodman, is spelled out in gold letters. Golda met him in Chicago, he was playing clarinet in the street, he was her neighbor, he had eleven brothers and sisters, a very poor Jewish family. To find him again, here in Eretz Israel, and with all they've been through along the way, is amazing to her. He left two tickets for Morris and her, and Morris seems delighted. The fact that Morris is here with her, that little Benny has become the king of swing, that this is happening in Haifa, and that she's sailing for America tomorrow: everything about this evening makes her feel emotional.

Backstage, among his musicians, Goodman has tears in his eyes when he sees her. She is lovely, laughing as she touches him with her hands like a child. Lost in the world, he feels he is from the same country as her. The hall is plunged in a semi-obscurity, and is so full that people are squeezed along the walls and even between the tables. Some are sitting on the floor at the edge of the space that will serve as a stage. The lights go out. At her table in the first row, Golda has her back to the audience, and there are no obstacles between her and the young musician. He looks at her as if he were getting ready to play for her alone, he lifts his clarinet to his lips and launches into a brilliant improvisation, immediately backed up by his musicians. The spectators remain strangely silent for minutes on end. They are listening to the dialogue between the instruments, and applaud in the wrong places. Golda is caught up in the rhythm and feels completely cut off from the audience. She was born in the ghetto in Kiev, and now here she is in the land of the Jews, by the sea, her arms open wide to welcome the return of the prodigal son. She is grateful, although she does not know to whom. Behind her, the approving murmur of the audience reinforces her feeling. It's an invisible echo chamber, a powerful, anonymous enhancement of her own sensation. The sound of swing, a serious yet light mystery, is beginning to have its effect on the audience: they let their emotions spill out the moment the first set is over. Even before the applause dies down, the clarinetist begins to work his magic, blowing with his lips: off he goes again. His breath causes the instrument to vibrate, a vibration propelled into the overheated air. The audience resonates, expands with the music, is carried by it, holds its breath and jumps up again with wild applause.

Golda senses someone looking at the back of her neck. From a precise spot in the dark hall, she has the impression that eyes are grazing over her shoulders, bristling the fine hairs at her nape. A feeling as light as a feather; she refuses to turn around, this tickling sensation is disturbing her, the music isn't the same anymore. She takes advantage of the ovation at the end of the next set to glance behind her. At the same moment a bright light floods the room then is instantly extinguished, a sort of atmospheric nightclub lighting. Even as darkness returns, the stroboscopic image persists, magnified on Golda's retina. The concert space is enormous, full to bursting, more of a dance hall than a jazz club, and the bay windows on all sides look out onto the sea. Most of the audience is Arab. Dignitaries from Haifa are sitting around large tables as if they were at a family dinner. There are many young people, children of the Palestinian middle class, and others of more modest origins. Party-goers, onlookers, women alone, eccentrics, music lovers. Several tables are filled with Jews speaking Arabic, speaking Hebrew, in couples or with their families. The hubbub fills Golda's ears. It has only taken a few seconds for the hall to fill, and to fill for her. At the heart of the vanished vision, in the split-second of brilliant light she has left behind, she can still see him, Albert Pharaon.

It's a hallucination. He is at a table just opposite the stage, his shoulders very straight, he is staring at her, ardently. He seems out of proportion in his suit, she hardly recognizes him, she's not in the habit of seeing him clothed. He seems to have gathered all his power about him. He is absolutely alone. His presence has an extraordinary intensity about it, devoted entirely to her.

Golda looks behind her again, she can't help it. Another flash of light, the dizzying hall seems to tip to one side, his chair is empty, Albert is a threatening shadow walking with a blind and determined gait toward one goal, Golda herself, sitting with Morris in the first row, a prisoner at her table, and Benny Goodman continuing to play all the while. A deathly chill rises the length of her spine and spreads across her shoulders. That step of her lover's: she recognizes it, she understands what is about to happen, nothing can stop it. He knew that their affair lived in fear of the light, he knew it! He came for that reason, deliberately, she is sure of it now, to watch her scorch her wings. He is only three yards away now, already lifting his arm. At the same time, the clarinet plays a few unusual notes in an alternating mode of acceleration and softness, a race between two principles, going faster and faster. Scattered applause greets the performance. The music shifts and sets off again, introducing new rhythms, mixing them with old ones, going up in stages, an endless to-and-fro, toward a point which could mean a culmination. Golda gets up and runs away from Albert. All the instruments are playing together now, and with the shouts of enthusiasm, the cries of "Bravo!," Morris hasn't noticed a thing, it's as if the entire hall were with Golda in her frenzied flight.

She escapes through the bay window and finds herself outside in the salty air. She turns around to face him, all her claws drawn. There is no one. Albert's dark figure has stayed by the door, a few yards behind her. He is coming toward her as if in a dream, in slow-motion. Around them the garden is deserted. The garlands of light make the place seem ghostly, unreal.

There is no one in the deck chairs lined up along the beach, no one at the café tables set under the trees. The brand new swimming pool, the playground, and the changing cabins are all deserted. The rolling of the waves is calming, but it is too dark to see the sea.

Albert touches Golda, she jumps back. Her face changes radically, distorted by a grimace of panic and disgust. She recoils like a hunted animal caught in a trap or on the verge of being struck by lightning. She is breathless, her throat has seized up, she cannot say a word. He understands that she is out of reach, on the far side, and that she has left the attraction behind. Or rather that he is the one who has gone beyond the attraction. He sees her in her organic reality, and the mirror she holds up to him glares with hurt. He has torn the screen, he is returning to the world. Golda stares at him with an almost indecent sharpness, an extreme weakness, as if she were seeking to imprint one last image. Her lover, very calm, turns on his heels and strides away.

13

From Germany - 1934

few yards behind him, some British soldiers who have appeared out of nowhere are pulling barriers into place to block off the wharf. Others are doing the same thing two hundred yards farther along. Albert finds himself an accidental captive. The new port of Haifa is another planet, a décor for giants. Standing there among the immense silos and hangars he feels as if he has shrunk. Everything has grown unfamiliar. Haifa itself has mushroomed. The modest seaside town has become one of the country's leading industrial centers, and the population is now one-third Jewish.

In the middle of the space enclosed by the barriers a ship is moored, a fairly big, sleepy-looking ship; it is impossible to tell whether it is transporting men or goods. There are soldiers standing around at regular intervals; men in civilian clothes make up a second circle, and others are setting up two long wooden tables on the wharf, where they are stacking piles of papers. Beneath the apparent liveliness of their activity, their gestures seem exhausted. A gaping hole opens in the side of the ship, from which men, women, and children slowly emerge. It is the first time that Albert has seen the immigrants at close hand, he is almost in their midst. The walking dead. It is as if the ground had opened beneath their feet and they began to fall and did not stop falling until they landed on this spot on the wharf. They move forward in slow motion, blinking, the same stunned absence visible on every face. But they have not massed together; they have not even had time to take on the uniformly gray color of refugees. Their clothes are rumpled but many of them are dressed tastefully, there are even some who still wear the veneer of Berlin aristocrats. Others seem to exude a dull suffering, with their long thin fingers, their gaunt faces and protruding cheekbones, their hollow gaze. Most are poor people, and yield more easily to submission, swept away on the tide like all the others.

"Which side are you on?"

A young British soldier asks him the question, aggressively. Albert doesn't quite understand, hesitates.

"Are you Jewish?"

"No."

"Then get to the other side of the barrier!"

Albert contemplates the Englishman's youth, his futile arrogance, his ignorance. In this place on this imaginary wharf, no one knows anymore who is who. Ever since he parted from Golda, everything around him is like that, dazed. The feeling of being a stranger never leaves him. He walks slowly to the other side of the barrier where the Arab dockers and porters are gathered. He stands among them. Their weathered skin smells of sweat and effort, their faces are closed. No one speaks, the tension is physically palpable, gathering the workers into one same mute body as they stare at the newcomers.

Behind the tables on the wharf, a young woman armed with a bullhorn is beginning a welcome speech in Hebrew, immediately translated into German by one of her companions. She is very young, and her tone is firm and clear. She says that after so much suffering and so much blindness the exiled people have at last arrived home, in this place where they have nothing more to fear. Those who have been seeking to forget their origins and lose themselves among others have had a bitter and cruel experience, but Eretz Israel will welcome those who strayed in the same way they welcome all the others, with open arms, provided they are Jewish. The people listening to her do not seem to understand. Distraught, isolated from each other, they seem so unbalanced that they forget where they are. The young woman goes on to deal with practical matters. She asks them to stand in line and prepare their documents. Next to Albert a somewhat elderly porter suddenly vaults over the barrier and, shouting and waving his hook, throws himself on the newcomers. He is alone, he is old, his efforts are laughable, but he is red with rage and his cry is so strangled that he seems close to collapse. Two British soldiers seize him without difficulty. As if it has all been choreographed, the young men in mufti slide their hands inside their jackets at the same time. All around Albert a collective cry of rage immediately rises on the air, a rough cry, fists raised, pure anger; a similar cry echoes in response from the dockers massed behind the other row of barriers, two hundred yards away. The echoing clamor now fuses above the heads of the immigrants: "Palestine is our land, the Jews are our dogs! With our blood, with our soul, we'll avenge you, our homeland!" Stones fly. Caught between two lines of fire, the German Jews don't know what is happening, don't know what to do. The stones fall around them. Some of them try to push their way back to the ship to find shelter, but most of them stay where they are, paralyzed.

An order rings out and the soldiers fire into the air. The burst of fire brings on the first signs of panic: the crowd of Arabs backs off a few yards. The soldiers use the opportunity to jump over the barriers and repel the rioters with the help of their rifle butts. One of the porters, a giant with white hair, fights back with every step. In broken English he screams at the advancing soldiers, saying the old fellow is his neighbor, he knows him, they have to let him go, he went crazy, what can you expect?

Albert shares this mixture of rage and helpless anger. He doesn't know where to direct it: not at the Jewish immigrants, nor even the British soldiers. The only one left is the young woman behind the table, so sure of herself, so blind, so Golda. And the situation itself: heart-wrenching, and so inextricable that it flares up on its own. He is carried by the ebbing crowd, and finally stops some hundred feet from the barriers. They are shouting again, *with our blood, with our blood*, and the stones are flying, but the immigrants are now out of reach.

Suddenly a very different clamor rings out. Albert watches as from between the hangars several dozen toughs, some of them in their undershirts, come running, brandishing clubs and shouting insults in Hebrew and Greek. These are the famous Jewish dockers "imported" from Salonika to run the Jewish traffic in the port of Haifa, and whose skirmishes with the Arab dockers regularly fill the columns of the newspapers. The soldiers rush to form a cordon between the two groups now heading for a fight. They also seem to be used to this. Jaws clenched, rifles across their chests, they meet the onslaught with whatever arrogance the British Empire still has in its possession. Albert stares at the young recruits, the absurdity of their position, this patch of wharf in the middle of nowhere, Jewish dockers, Arab dockers, Jewish immigrants, Palestine, and these British soldiers caught in the middle wondering what the dickens they are doing there. The Jewish dockers come to a halt a few yards from the uniforms, shouting threats, waving their clubs; the Arab dockers brandish their hooks and give as good as they get, Arabic mingling with Greek and Hebrew, the same scene being played out behind the other barriers two hundred yards away, giving the impression of an infinitely reproducible situation. The German Jews wait in the no-man's land between the barriers, forgotten, lost, suspended above all geography.

In the venerable hall of the Pharaon bank, a strange couple stand waiting for Albert beneath the chandelier. Everything is like this nowadays, details slipping into the most familiar settings and casting doubt upon their coherence. The man is in his thirties, with a threadbare suit, hollow cheeks, a febrile gaze; the woman, very young and tall and almost bony, in a tight-fitting dress made of colored pieces of fabric stitched together. She has very short black hair, angular features, dark eyes, a dusky landscape marked in the middle by large red lips. Employees and clients are stepping around them; some later era has, by accident, burst in upon their own.

"Are you Mr. Pharaon?" asks the man.

His voice is gentle, a German accent.

"Yes, I am."

The man gives him an intense smile and his face lights up. In one instant his grave and painful expression has become almost naïve. His name is Emil Stein, he used to do theater set design in Munich, her name is Ada, she was a dance teacher. They arrived in Palestine three months ago. It was not their choice, but the rest of the world was closed to them. Albert invites them into his office. The young woman walks ahead of him. Nothing in her allure connects her to anything familiar. She seems to stumble and catch herself with each step, her long arms swinging on either side of her body to keep her balance, her grace is improbable, and yet obvious. Her companion follows her, as calm and stable as she is apparently chaotic. As soon as he is seated, Emil Stein opens a tin box that he has been holding against his chest and pulls out a wad of banknotes:

"One thousand seven hundred and fifty dollars. Luckily, we changed them before the mark fell."

His tone is both modest and solemn, as is his gesture as he places the notes on the desk. Ada on the other hand seems very restless; she cannot sit still, looks all around her, a groundless anxiety in her eyes. They are like two opposites making one couple, the poles of a magnet repelling one another. Albert never has anything to do with business at the bank, but this is clearly something else:

"What is the matter?" he asks.

Emil Stein breathes a sigh of relief and leans back to be more comfortable. Ada's eyes cease their restless interrogation of the walls and focus on Albert. For the first time he hears the young woman's voice, hoarse, warm, foreign, breaking from time to time:

"Back there, they reproached us for being Jews, and here we are obliged to be Jewish: there's no solution. But there has to be one."

"I really wish there were one," says Albert.

"For us, depositing our money with you is a beginning," murmurs Emil.

"I'm not sure I understand."

Emil explains, his words tumbling over each other. Germany had been a giant workshop, everyone was laboring in his corner to invent modern times and no one asked who was Jewish and who wasn't. Then the theaters closed, and the dance classes, there was no more money and sometimes nothing to eat. They had just had a child, a boy they call Hugo. Everywhere you looked, there was a crisis. And yet they kept going, just differently, you couldn't just stop, but the ferocious hostility around them was getting ever stronger. Inadvertently, Ada mimics the feelings which Emil's story reawakens in her. Golda had the same face one evening, all the lights of the past beamed onto her skin. The two women have absolutely nothing in common, he might even say that they are complete opposites. And yet Albert is troubled when he recognizes in Ada that same capacity to make her body a conduit. Golda's image, the image of that impossible thing named Golda, merges with that of the young German woman across from him whose lips are moving silently. Emil Stein is saying that the world they once belonged to hung by a thread, and that the thread has broken. Her words struggling past her throat, Ada inhales deeply to try to calm herself. Albert holds out his packet of cigarettes. The three of them sit silently smoking in the big office.

"It's when we arrived here that we became Jews," continues Emil in a strangled voice. "Of course we were Jews there too, already, but we despised being classified in that way by the enemy, it was something they wanted. In Palestine, we no longer have that luxury. They've been kind to us, and welcoming, and efficient, and it's true that without them I don't know how we would have managed. But the way they spoke to us was a constant reminder of our own mistake: we thought we were Germans, but in fact we were only Jews. They would look at us as if we'd been ashamed of being Jews, and it was driving us crazy. As if the Nazis' victory in the elections was proof that the Jews had to leave the world and live together in one single ghetto."

"There aren't only Jews in this country," says Albert.

"I am making my living as a foreman in construction, and most of the workers are Arabs, we use sign language. But they don't exist. They build houses for the Jews and then they disappear as if they'd never been there. Ada and I are living in one of those houses, in the eastern part of Haifa, a row of little buildings that all look alike. To keep from suffocating we've developed the habit of going to the Old Town to wander around, where the streets and the houses go a long way back. We've been looking for you for a long time, Mr. Pharaon."

Ada's smile creases her face. Emil is just as mischievous. Both of them, suddenly, seem to be playing a good joke on life.

"We saw your building, we just stood there in front of it," continues Emil. "A bank called Pharaon—you can't make that up. The façade, the arcades, the stone work, it was all so real! We came in, you weren't here. We saw the carpets and the chandeliers, the employees, the clients, the sort of indolent animation in the offices . . . We got the feeling we actually were somewhere."

"You are fortunate," replies Albert with a laugh. "Because you see, I personally don't know very well where I am."

Emil Stein laughs with him, as does Ada. Then they fall silent but this time, it is as if their silence has loosened the knot.

"I'm not a believer and religion is nothing to me," adds Emil. "But there is a story in the Bible that I like, the one about Joseph persecuted by his brothers so he runs away and finally finds refuge in the land of the pharaohs."

Albert laughs, but this time with an emotion that surprises him and only intensifies when he sees that his visitor has tears in his eyes. As for Ada, when she sees the affliction in her husband's eyes she is filled with panic.

"If you are free tonight," says Albert, "come to my place for dinner. I live in an old house on Mount Carmel. A dream house, but a very real one at the same time. You'll see, you'll like it there."

14

Modern Times - 1935

The first time they came to dinner, Ada was not even able to sit down at the table that was set out in the garden; she began to feel her hackles rise. It was too much, too solemn for her, to the point of obscenity. Her large red lips formed around the word, obscene, and it brought tears to her eyes. She had a violent argument with Emil. Albert went to find Najjar to ask him to remove everything, the starched tablecloth, the crystal glasses. On his way back to the garden, he could hear their outbursts. Ada's voice became so shrill that it was on the verge of breaking. It was as if something or someone were shouting through her throat; it was almost frightening. Albert held back, behind the glass door. He saw Emil get up and leave the house.

Ada turned to face the black hole of the Bay of Haifa and did not move. Her narrow shoulders were shaking. Albert went up to her. He did not know what to do, so he did nothing. She eventually turned to him, her eyes perfectly dry, although they seemed larger. In a very low voice she said she was sorry, that this kind of argument between Emil and herself had become frequent since they came to Palestine. As if feeling her way, she placed her forehead on Albert's chest. He remained motionless, as did she, with this sole point of contact. She stepped back only after a long pause. With slow gestures, as if something were holding him back, he opened a bottle. They sat drinking.

Then she went on a tour of the house. Albert walked behind

her, it was extraordinary, she brought each room alive. The walls, the proportions, the open windows: everything seemed to please her, to speak to her. It was not just that she liked the house; it was that she felt at home there, miraculously. She acknowledged with gratitude this place where she had never been. She touched the smooth stone and let her fingers run over it for the pleasure. Never had the house felt as truly inhabited as it did on that evening, by virtue of a young woman's grace. They had dinner on the lawn. She refused to leave. Somewhat drunk, she said that this place now belonged to her. Albert asked Najjar to prepare the guest room.

He felt her slide into his bed, her naked legs against his. She was wearing the pajama top that he had lent her. She pushed her head down under the covers. Her long body was nothing more than a motionless shape. Dawn was beginning to illuminate the edges of the curtains. She had turned her face to him. Her black eyes shone in the semi-darkness, as if the light were beaming from them. Albert suggested they go and make some tea. She looked at him without moving. He had tried to slip past her body. In the midst of his gesture Ada had thrown off the covers and encircled him tightly with her arms and legs. She had incredible strength; he would never have suspected she was so muscular.

The soft red smile on her face at that moment, as if she were dreaming. Albert remembers the moment she raised herself up to take off her pajama top, revealing breasts that were surprisingly full on such a slim body. He recalls the slowness of their gestures, the shivering of their limbs, the velvety feel of her forbidden skin. For a long time it was soft and shivery, then suddenly Ada changed, her dry smooth body went wild. An obscure, foreign force took over, and you couldn't tell whether it was a benign one or not, it raised her up like a puppet, as if to contort her limbs. She responded with ferocious strength, letting her hips take over, opening her arms, dancing. All the demons in her belly were aroused. Albert was overwhelmed. Ada's thighs gripped like steel around his pelvis. He was a fixed point. But she was moving like an enraged mare, a wild animal, rearing above him. She was shouting as if she had to expel the nightmare inside her, to spit it out, get rid of it for good. And she was pushing, seeking, her arms reaching for the sky, her pubis desperately thrust forward and her eyes full of tears, she couldn't do it, she began over and over until at last came the final improbable spasm, the magnificent and painful culmination. Albert remembers. This first embrace was followed by more peaceable ones, and time lost all meaning. He remembers her parted lips, her irregular but patient breathing, her dark, faintly veiled eyes which would not let him go even when the pleasure was slowly imminent. They had finally managed to part:

"From now on," she had said, her voice low, "you are my Palestinian lover."

The very next day Ada opened the Pink House. She brought Emil with her, and all their friends. The luxurious residence became a world, Ada's world. Germany had arrived at Albert's place. The visitors would come through the door, and some of them did not even know who he was. Day after day, his ears were ringing with the words of a tragedy and an imagined world he did not know, even as another tragedy was unfolding before their eyes. Chance had set him at the crossroads between two universes, and he was looking out on all sides— and he saw Ada. She alone gave a sense of unity. The way she moved enraptured him. She would go from one guest to another, flowing, transparent, creating ties without even realizing it. She was the center and the outsider all at the same time, a strange mixture. She never looked at Albert, her eyes grazed over him, eyelashes lowered. She would talk to him, smile at him, only sidelong glances. In public, she was absent, as far as he was concerned. Emil held no grudges against Albert, he looked him straight in the eye. No one was deceived. Emil loved Ada, knew how fragile she was, and wanted only to protect the equilibrium she was finding.

Nothing was preventing Albert from giving himself to this love. He hardly dared believe it, but believed it all the same: the future was full of promise, he had become desirable. Like a famished soul too long deprived of hope, he felt a boundless euphoria welling up inside. And what if it was these rootless German Jews who were about to become the stimulus he had sought in vain until now? Why shouldn't they? They were not Zionists, and they had no dreams of a separate society. Misfortune had obliged them to seek refuge in an Arab world that they did not reject: why couldn't they transform it? Some German Jews had already founded an organization, Brit Shalom, for the creation of a bi-national Judeo-Arab state. The original Zionist utopia was finally beginning to show itself for what it was: unattainable. Palestine had one chance to come out of its long sleep and become a viable nation. A small inner voice continued to tell him that he was dreaming, that the mass arrival of these German Jews was viewed by Palestinian society as a mortal threat. But Albert no longer listened to that little voice. He was too content. Ada was there before his eyes. He watched her walk across the garden and did not dare disturb her. And he shivered when he thought that that very evening, perhaps, she would be in his arms.

Without even realizing it, Albert has progressively adopted the weekly rhythm of the Sabbath. None of his visitors pray, none of them bless the bread and the wine, but they all work for Jewish companies and the faint holiday air that reigns on that particular day even among the staunchest non-believers has ended up affecting Albert as well. It's the Sabbath. Today, in the middle of the afternoon, his guests are playing chess or lying under the trees in the garden. They knew each other in Germany. New arrivals crop up frequently. Each wave of immigration seems linked to a tragic event: there are those who gave up after the first looting of Jewish shops, or the first auto-dafés, or the racial laws of Nuremberg, or the burnings of the synagogues. In any case, they had no more work. In the first year alone after the Nazis took power, half the German Jews became unemployed. When they left they asked friends or neighbors to look after their houses and their belongings, but with each passing week those same friends and neighbors had to leave in turn. Each wave of arrivals is proof of the worsening situation, and at the same time brings Palestine that little bit closer to the edge. In this headlong rush toward the abyss, the Pink House and its garden perched on a cliff above the bay have become a refuge. The lush vegetation is left to run riot, and the open sky gives them a sense of freedom. Only Ada ventures into the house's interior. She comes and goes, no one asks her a thing, Emil observes her from a distance.

The inseparable Meyer brothers appear at the garden gate. They are the ghosts of their former selves, pale, trembling, their clothes in a mess.

"Who is this Ezzeddin el-Qassam?" they shout.

Everyone gathers around them, they are covered in dust.

"We almost got lynched as we were leaving Tel Aviv. Hooligans were setting tires on fire and they took over the streets, they had keffiehs hiding their faces, they hurled stones at the bus. They were shouting in Arabic, we couldn't understand a thing. We managed to make our way through the columns of smoke. But once we got to the main square in Haifa our bus got stuck in a crowd of people that was turning into a riot, and people just kept coming from every side street. We couldn't go forward or back, they shattered the windows with stones. The driver told us to lie down between the seats. Men, women, children, Jews with side curls, even a few Arabs, everybody screaming, praying, crying. The rioters were trying to tip the bus over and it was rocking harder and harder, even when the British soldiers came in to get us out. And they just kept shouting that name at the top of their lungs, Ezzeddin el-Qassam! Ezzeddin el-Qassam! Who is he?"

"He's a sheik preacher who was killed by the British a few days ago," says Albert. "They buried him today in Haifa. For years he's been going from village to village trying to convince the landless peasants to wage a holy war against the Jews and the British. He had three kibbutzniks and two Jewish farmers killed. When the grand mufti refused to join him in launching a call to insurrection, he decided to do it on his own. He set up his lair in the Samaria mountains. With a few partisans, he spent twenty days fleeing from cave to cave. The British eventually hunted him down, but he refused to turn himself in. So they killed him, which is about the worst thing they could have done."

"Why?"

"Because three days ago he was completely unknown. Nothing more than a little local terrorist leader. But to die like that, with his weapon in his hand, that's what makes a legend. For three days, they have been shouting his name at spontaneous demonstrations in every town in the country."

There is something unreal about it. The guests look at each other. They understand what it means when the moment comes for a nation paralyzed with rage to break their bonds and spill out into the street. They know that this sudden shift has every chance of causing the ground beneath their feet to tremble, but they have no control over such an event. Everything is happening in a faraway country also known as Palestine. Only the Meyer twins, sitting on the edge of the fountain, have any concrete understanding of the danger.

"I have good news," says Albert. "You'll be able to go to Amman."

The emotion on the faces of the two brothers is all the stronger for the way in which it instantly dissolves their fear. They get to their feet and take Albert in their arms. They were both architects with the Bauhaus in Berlin. Without a whisper of protest they left behind their passion for stark simple houses in order to come and plane planks and drive nails in Palestine. They have become carpenters in Tel Aviv. And now the Emir Abdullah has entrusted them with the cabinetry for the palace he is building in Amman. One of Albert's friends has been acting as an intermediary.

The buzzing of insects and the barking of dogs in the distance seem to amplify the silence. Palm trees sway on the hillside. Everything is so calm. Ada approaches, no one notices. Her jaw is trembling, as if she were frozen:

"I'm a bad Jew, no Jew at all!" she cries in her throaty voice. "I refuse to learn Hebrew, I won't stay here. Whatever country will give me a visa, that will be my country. My language is dance. I'll go anywhere, I'll give classes while I wait until I can go back to Munich. The Nazi regime won't last forever, I'm only twenty-two!"

Ada is standing by the fountain, her arms loose at her side, all alone and somehow apart from the others. The setting sun lingers on her bony figure, her bare legs, her brightly colored dress. The others can talk, get carried away, give voice to the torment of their life. Ada says nothing, unless it is to shout. Her body is free, full of pain, full of tension, and it is her body which incarnates all her contradictions. She represents modernity at the same time as she represents its failure. Albert would like to take her in his arms.

15

The Funeral - 1936

Albert was on his way from Jerusalem to Haifa when the car had a puncture. The place was deserted, a little country road that wound its way down between the hills. There was nothing for it but to change the tire, and he wasn't sure he'd manage. A family of Arab peasants appeared in the road as if out of nowhere. Like a mirage. The man wearing his jellaba and keffieh, the mother holding a baby wrapped in a blanket, and a boy who might have been ten or so walking along behind them. Their tattered clothing flapping in the wind. They stopped in silence a short distance from the car. Albert greeted them before asking if there was a village nearby. They didn't answer, it was as if they didn't understand the language. Albert got back to work. The man came closer, silently and slowly, the others followed. Standing very straight, as if before history, he introduced himself and said the name of the village of his origins. He spoke a very pure, classical Arabic. The baby had just had an operation in Jerusalem and now they were going back to their village, on foot. He fell silent. Somewhat surprised, Albert asked where their village was located. The man indicated a spot in the mountains that would involve a detour of fifteen miles or so.

The family were standing a dozen feet or more from Albert, but even at that distance, he could smell the odor—thick cloth that had never been washed, sweat, animals and poverty. It made your stomach heave. The woman was speaking behind the man's back, the child was still sick, it needed to rest and the road was long. Albert was about to suggest he would give them a ride when the man pulled a filthy handkerchief from his jellaba and untied it with a royal gesture to reveal what it contained: a few silver coins. Ill at ease, Albert made a gesture to shrug it off before placing his hand on his heart and opening the doors of the car. A terrible expression on his face, the man raised his hand to stop his family from stepping forward, the other hand still holding the open handkerchief. Each gesture was transformed into its opposite. Albert said loudly that he was offended, even insulted. How could he accept to be paid for a favor offered to a brother? The woman began to cry, she begged her husband to swallow his pride and accept the stranger's generous offer. Albert knew it would not be long before he would have to implore the man in order to get him to agree to ride in the car. He was still standing in the middle of the road, his face closed, his hand outstretched, stubbornly entrenched. Tired of insisting, Albert closed the handkerchief over the coins and, holding it with two fingers, took it with him to the dashboard.

The road to the hamlet was a mere rutted, stony track which faded in and out between the hills. The stench was so strong that even with the windows wide open the air was impossible to breathe. The man was sitting in front, the woman and children behind. The baby wasn't crying. It was dead. That is what the man confessed to Albert, in a broken voice. The operation did not go smoothly at the hospital, in fact, there was no hospital at all. The child had died, never mind how, and they were taking it back to the village to be buried. Albert stopped the car on the shoulder of the road. He looked at the father, the little boy, the mother holding her bundle of rags, he touched their hands. He told them he would stay with them for the burial. A tear fell across the man's weathered cheek. With an embarrassed and shameful gesture he wrapped up the coins that were still on the dashboard and stuffed them deep into his jellaba.

Albert stood in the front row at the funeral, next to the men of the family. Behind them walked twenty or so peasants, mute with sorrow. The women followed, striking their breasts, keening. A primitive scene taking place in the present. The same ritual, the same sun-scorched landscape, the same cries. But the sorrow on that day was unbearable, caused by death and by the evidence of a life which had not been lived, a non-life, a non-existent future.

The hamlet numbered no more than a dozen houses, the cemetery formed a small square at the top of the hill. The tears and wailing had increased in volume. The grave was tiny, the smells which rose from it were intoxicating. Earth. Albert felt physically both the sensuality and the dampness of it; the very substance of history. Their palms open, held before them like a book, the peasants recited the Fatiha, the first verse of the Koran, "You whom we adore, We implore Your help." Their mournful mumbling was muted by the shrill lamentations, male and female, mingling into one chant. Standing there by the grave, surrounded by affliction, Albert suddenly understood that Ada had nothing to do with this country. She had not come to this land because she desired it, her destiny was not inextricably linked to that of the land. This dark intoxication, of a person's relationship with their life and their death, was not something for Ada—and never would be.

He returned to Haifa a zombie; the car seemed to drive itself. He had not slept all night. He was obsessed by the disappearance of Ada's image. And then? And then Golda. He had spent the night driving her from his mind. It was something he had always known, and knew now: Golda alone was bound in that organic way to this earth. She would never leave. Come what may, her attachment to the land would be as strong as the peasants'. She was the obvious key, but a broken key that would open onto nothing, only suffering and broken hearts. In a flash of understanding Albert admitted that he was bound to her forever, condemned for life. Because she, Golda, was the one that he loved. And with her it was impossible.

He woke up in the middle of the afternoon, fully dressed, lying cross-wise on the bed. Ada was bending over him, it took him several instants to recognize her. She was asking what was wrong, whether he was sick. He shook his head, his tongue was coated, a headache confused his mind. It all came back at once. With infinite sadness he put his arms around the young woman's neck and held her to him. She did not even seem surprised.

He got up and led her out onto the west-facing terrace, the one she liked. She let him lead her there, no questioning glances or words. Her presence was calming. On the terrace Albert told her the whole story, his illusion and the role she had played in it, the dead child, the funeral, his love for Golda. At the same time he wept. She had never seen him cry. Curled up with her arms around her knees, she listened with a rare intensity, without getting flustered. Her calm at that moment seemed symmetrical to her usual craziness.

What did he think? That they could live happy, stable lives, the two of them? The way they were, with this country around them? A sweet love story in the tiny circles of German Jewish immigrants? In any case, it would not have lasted. She could only love him and thank him for the light-hearted days, the stolen days he had given her. Thank him too on behalf of the others, those he had welcomed unquestioningly to his peaceful refuge of a house. His welcome had been all the more extraordinary in that it was free and unconscious at the same time. What would he do now? Put an end to this experience, this shared life? Find himself alone again to watch while his country went under? Spend his time wallowing in the love he bore an unattainable woman? She spoke as if she were gambling her life; she stood very straight now, full of rage, her feet planted firmly on the ground and her head tilting skyward. Albert's heart was pounding. The future remained just as dark, but Ada was offering him light. Then she fell silent, all of a sudden. Her body relaxed as she let out a long sigh, she blushed, smiled, her eyes two slits, almost closed. For a long time she looked at Albert through her lashes:

"Your house must remain open," she murmured.

"You and I . . . "

"I know, you can't anymore. It's a pity. We won't sleep together anymore."

The friends continued to come. Life went on as before, except for Ada, who constantly stole glances at Albert, her eyes following him everywhere. Emil, gently, drew closer to her. Albert was very grateful for the existence of this world around him, it was saving his life. But his attention was elsewhere. He contemplated the events shaking the country with a gaze that was empty and enthralled at the same time. He no longer thought in political terms. The occasionally violent strikes organized by the Arabs seemed to him to be a protest against the impossibility of living together, a pathetic plea to be seen and taken into account at last, the dark expression of a lover's pique. He read in life what he read in his heart. He liked being alone, and for there to be noise outside. They left him alone. Ada made sure of that, without anyone realizing, Albert even less so than anyone. He lived like this month after month, and they all lived with him. He did not think of Golda in particular, but she was there all the time. Her image was burned onto his retina, she drifted through his mind and emerged in his thoughts without warning, a knife blade.

16

GOLDA - 1937

Najjar follows her like a ghost. Her black hair bobs on her shoulders, her step is lively. She is beautiful, strong—beautiful because of her strength. Albert gets up and goes to meet her. She is wearing a short-sleeved flowered dress, clutching a little handkerchief in her fingers; there is an air of spring about her. Her image shimmers in the heat, the breeze plays with the hem of her dress, he would recognize her among thousands just from the way she moves. He shakes his head to gather his wits about him; no, there can be no doubt. It really is her. He looks at her as if nothing could satisfy his hunger to see her, he has missed her so terribly, it is all such a surprise. She says softly:

"You are so pale and upright, and you've lost weight."

As for Golda, her features seem more clearly defined, thicker, more intense; he has no desire to tell her so. An old smile from long ago rises to his lips:

"How are you?" he asks, simply.

"I've moved, I'm living alone with my children. These past six months I've been kissing them goodbye in the morning not knowing if I'd see them again in the evening. The road from Tel Aviv to Jerusalem has become the most dangerous road in the country. One stone, one shot, a bomb . . . it can all happen so quickly."

She falls silent. He would have liked for her to go on, just to hear the familiar sound of her voice again. With a dazed gesture, he invites her to sit down. She walks by him and stops.

She raises her eyes, her hand, to his face. Very slowly, she traces his features with her fingertips. The exact same gesture, long ago. He doesn't move. Her hand falls, she forgets to step back. They stand there for a long time, breathing each other in. Albert does not know if he can touch this woman, if he knows her again. He is not sure he wants to know. She came, that is the main thing. For the time being, he likes this immobility.

"And you?" she asks, almost touching his chest.

"Nothing. I read the papers, I listen to the radio, the conflict is unfolding beneath my windows. I would never have believed the Palestinians could keep this strike going for six months. They are becoming a nation before my eyes. I have no desire to go anywhere, I spend my time arguing with you."

She laughs. She steps aside. Her face regains its composure. Whatever was vague has vanished from her eyes: she has come with a precise purpose. He puts his hand on her mouth to stop her from speaking, she looks at him with astonishment. He bends his knees and sits down in the grass, pulls her down with him. Let her simply come and see the Pink House, the garden, the surrounding landscape, he asks nothing else. He knows nothing is possible, his body tells him as much. But their mutual attraction is intact. It's a dizziness, a long suspension. The shadows of solitary clouds pass over the city at the foot of the hill. Jews and Arabs are catching their breath, tending their wounds, perhaps they are dreaming. Albert feels no different from them. He does not really have any hope. He is simply grateful that there is a respite from the violence—and that Golda is next to him, miraculously. He would like to turn to her and kiss her. She would respond by biting him on the lip. Their lips would be red, they would sharpen their gaze in each other's eyes. He would have tasted her, would have made sure of her material self, that is all he might want.

"I've come to tell you that things may become very dangerous in Haifa."

He scarcely hears her. His gaze wanders over the texture of her skin, the curve of her neck, the rise and fall of her chest. He is looking for the woman he once knew. This woman looks a great deal like her, it is almost her. Golda takes him by the shoulders and shakes him gently:

"The British Commission has informed us of its conclusions: the partition of Palestine into a Jewish state for one-third of the country, and an Arab state for the rest. No Jews in the Arab state, no Arabs in the Jewish state. The British might have to take charge of the forced transfer of populations. Jerusalem will have an international status, and Haifa will become entirely Jewish."

Golda's lips are moving, her eyes are staring at him, her expression is one of incredible determination. Everything seems to indicate that she has become a woman of power. Albert can scarcely believe a word she is saying. How can this be possible? The Arabs in Galilee and Haifa would just pick up their things and abandon their homes because the Jews want to live on their own? And if they don't, the British would come along and evacuate them *manu militari?* And the Jews would be offered *one-third* of the country, emptied out for them ahead of time?

Down in the port a liner is maneuvering to find its berth among the ships moored along the waterfront. This familiar landscape is as tangible to Albert as the wind on his skin, the smell of the scrub on the hillside, the humming of the crickets. What is real? he wonders. Golda is looking hard at him:

"The six months of strikes among the Arabs that you seem to be so proud of have actually been a blessing for us. Every Palestinian who stopped work was replaced by a Jew. All the events have played in our favor. We've prepared the structure of a Jewish state, beyond our wildest hopes, and it will be vital the day that war breaks out in Europe."

"Why did you come to see me, Golda?"

"There are Jewish groups who are getting ready to start a war in Haifa. You have no idea how violent they are. Look out for yourself."

She gets to her feet, her eyes lowered. For the first time, Albert is touched. He can tell that Golda is afraid for him. She has lost her mask of self-assurance and sovereignty; her expression is troubled. For a few seconds, he has found her, recognizes her. He has no time to react. She has turned her head, and she has already fled.

17

ADA - 1937

The explosion is definitely louder than usual, the windows of the Pink House rattle. Albert goes out into the garden just as the next one comes. Two enormous columns of smoke are visible in the lower town. There is the wailing of ambulance sirens. The sound of machine guns has become background noise and no longer even disrupts conversation. He switches on the radio: the first bomb exploded in the melon market in the middle of the crowd, the second in the vegetable market. The hospitals are besieged. It is the work of Irgun Jewish extremists, and this is their fourth attack on Haifa.

Someone is knocking on the door. Najjar is absent. Albert goes to open. It is Ada, white with fear, her son Hugo in her arms. A long bloody streak crosses her chest from her shoulder to her hip, almost in a straight line. Her eyes are bulging, and through clenched teeth she says,

"We're all right, the two of us, we weren't touched. It's someone else's blood!"

"Come in."

The terrified child clings to his mother's neck and she clings to him. Albert leads them hastily into a room and closes the shutters. No sooner does his head hit the pillow than Hugo falls into a semi-conscious state. He is moaning, punching and kicking the void. Kneeling by his bed, Ada tries to calm him by holding his shoulders and speaking to him in German. Albert waits behind her in the semi-darkness. Soon he hears nothing but Ada's murmurs. The exhausted child has fallen asleep. The young woman continues to speak to him, more and more quietly. She stays on her knees with her forehead on the blankets, and finally lets out a long sigh that ends in a startled, nervous tremor.

Communication with Amman is poor, and Albert has to speak more loudly than he would have liked. He hangs up and goes to look one last time through the crack in the door. Ada is still asleep, Hugo too. Emil is sitting by their side, lost in thought. He came running, his face covered in paint, looking like a real worker. Albert pushes the door slightly and motions to him. Emil stands up. Ada senses this and seizes his hand. She pulls away from her son and gets to her feet. Emil holds her. Walking awkwardly, she goes out into the garden. The late afternoon sunshine is still warm. She realizes she has slept all day. She sits down in a wicker chair, her back to the town.

Najjar comes out with some refreshments. Still incapable of speaking English, he mimes the gestures to convey to the young woman and her companion the sorrow he feels.

"Are you ready to leave the country?" asks Albert.

"Without hesitation," replies Emil.

18

1948

Najjar closes the gate behind him and catches his breath. The bright colors of the garden reassure him, the fragrance of fermenting vegetation gives him a slight dizzy feeling, springtime is bursting with life. Were it not for the storm of war, he might believe that he too is surrounded by this overripe vegetable peace, ready to explode with the rising of the sap. He is forty years old but his expression remains childlike. He goes from one room to the other looking for Albert. The electricity is back on. The radio goes from one news story to the next, and no one is listening. Najjar feels alone in the world. He goes back out into the garden, agitated. Albert is nowhere to be found. Finally he spots him sitting beyond the row of trees overlooking the town and the port.

"Monsieur Albert, I thought you'd been abducted!"

Albert's temples are white, the years have sharpened his features and worn a groove between his eyebrows. He doesn't seem to hear. His attention is wandering among the plumes of smoke rising from the center of town and the southeastern suburb of Haifa. He is elegant as always but has lost so much weight that his suit floats on him. His skin is like parchment, his frail figure seems ready to dissolve in thin air. He is deeply upset by *what happened*. There's no other way to say it: What happened. His mind is not big enough. Ghosts, writhing in pain, millions of them, Ada and Emil's families annihilated, and all of their loved ones. He has not seen Golda for eleven years. He wrote to her, *I am with you, I am thinking about you*, feeble words. She didn't answer. Golda, the love story he had with her, Palestine, everything has faded.

With his awkward gestures, Najjar opens his canvas bag and empties the contents onto the ground.

"Lobster in a can, cream of asparagus, button mushrooms, Swiss chocolate, Italian spaghetti, cherries in Armagnac, two bottles of French wine and a bottle of whisky aged twelve years."

The oddness of the inventory eventually arouses Albert: "Where did you find all that?"

"Across the way, at Mr. Boutagy's."

"His villa has been closed for months."

Najjar blushes. He touches one of the cans:

"A shell made a hole right by the kitchen, God forgive me."

"But that's looting," says Albert, with a faraway smile.

"Do you think so?" murmurs Najjar, suddenly anxious.

"Let's call it war booty, rather."

He falls silent, tired from the effort of speaking. But Najjar seems so distraught that he makes one last effort:

"Taking over the supplies of deserters is perfectly moral, and I think the whisky will do."

A torrent of violent explosions shakes the ground, a salvo of a dozen or more bursts of fire, the house seems to be taking a direct hit. Najjar throws himself to the ground, Albert folds himself in half on his chair. Silence returns. They look around them. There is no visible destruction, no broken glass, no fire. The house is intact, the garden basks in the sun. But plumes of smoke mushroom below them in the old town, far down the hillside, followed by the delayed echo of the impact.

"It's coming from behind the house," says Albert. "Those are the mortars the Haganah set up on the summit of Mount Carmel. This time I think the conquest of Haifa is under way once and for all."

Najjar, astonished to be alive, gets back to his feet, his face as white as his jellaba:

"But why now?"

"This morning the British General Stockwell announced that he refused to take responsibility for the town."

"What does that mean?"

"That means that the Haganah have their hands free to come and get us however they like."

A new series of explosions provides an answer, as terrifying as the first time. Najjar dives nose first back into the dust and begins to shout:

"Monsieur Albert, what are we going to do?"

"Don't be afraid, the shells are going over our head. There's no danger for the time being."

"All the same, we can't stay here!"

"I can. But you, you're Egyptian, you have nothing to do with this war. You should leave."

"Of course I should leave, everyone's leaving. With all due respect, Monsieur Albert, you really don't know what's going on anymore. The Jews have a real army now, with tanks. They won the battle of Castel and the road to Jerusalem is open to them. Jaffa, Tiberiad, and Safed are besieged, Haifa too. There's no one left to defend us. The city will fall. In Deir Yassin two hundred and forty-five men, women and children were massacred by the Irgun last week."

"The Lebanese border is only an hour away on foot. I'll give you some money and an address in Beirut. If you knew how to drive I'd have given you the car."

"But what about you?"

"It disgusts me. All the bankers and landowners and politicians took off and left all the poor people behind, and they're running around like chickens with their heads cut off."

"But what will change if you stay behind?"

"Nothing. I just don't feel like finding myself on the road in the middle of a flood of refugees. I have a front row seat here. I think I'm staying because I'm too tired for anything else."

*

The mortars finally fell silent at dawn, and every moment of silent calm seems like a blessing. Najjar is still waiting. He has swapped his jellaba for a checked shirt and a pair of pants and feels like a stranger to himself. The street leading down the hillside is deserted, and smells of sulfur and burning. He moves slowly forward through the rubble, the twisted pylons, the electric wires dangling over the road. Where is everyone? The city is strangely absent of voices; even the birds are silent.

At the edge of the town center forms begin to appear, ghosts passing one another with uncomprehending gazes. After the night they have spent, they leave their homes with an uncertain step and discover the changed aspect of their street. Even though they look like the walking dead, their presence reassures Najjar. From one minute to the next they grow more numerous. No one is speaking, the silence is as thick as fog. A solitary whistling suddenly rips through the air, followed by an explosion some fifty yards away. The burst of flame illuminates their faces. The people jump, rush back, look at the sky, motionless, waiting for what comes next. No shells, no sound, only a faint breeze sweeping with it an aftertaste of smoke. Very slowly the ghost-like inhabitants begin to move again down the middle of the street. Najjar wonders if he should not leave them behind and hurry on his way. But he stays with them, overcome by their strange collective passivity.

A distant rumbling can be heard, the clanking of a tracked vehicle accompanied by isolated bursts of fire.

"Here come the tanks, the Jews are coming!"

The shout shatters their inertia. In a matter of seconds a wave of panic arouses the neighborhood. People rush back to their houses and come back out weighted down with their children, suitcases, bundles, mattresses, kitchen utensils, and all the bric-a-brac that have always made up their lives. Entire families suddenly fill the streets, with dozens of children. "The Jews are coming!" The rumble of tanks grows louder, the shots seem to be coming more frequently. It would seem that the Arabs of Haifa have pulled out the few weapons they still have at their disposal. Shells burst in isolated spots, no one pays any attention. The panic-stricken men and women have only one thought: to flee as quickly as possible.

Najjar has left before them. Instead of carrying on in the direction of the port, he takes a turn-off to the right to look for a way out of town that would enable him to reach Lebanon via the back roads. Five hundred yards farther along he catches sight of a column of the Haganah headed directly toward him. The sight of the armored vehicles and the Jewish soldiers looking somewhat disheveled in their uniforms draws him up short: for the first time, he feels that this is real. Never has he run so quickly in all his life. The street he left behind only moments before is unrecognizable. Despite the bombs and the artillery fire, a sizeable crowd has spilled onto the pavement, pushing, pulling, shouting, turning on itself in an endless whirlwind. Which way should he go? "There's no way out, we're trapped!" shouts someone. "The road to the port is still open!" shouts someone else, and the crowd rushes off in that direction, blindly. Najjar does not even have time to decide, he is carried away by the human torrent.

A bit farther along he veers off into Allenby Street, which is completely paralyzed. The crowd is crushed against stopped vehicles—cars, carts, bicycles, horses, buses piled up with suitcases and human beings of all ages. It quickly becomes unbearable to be caught in the mass. Some keep their dignity but most of the fleeing crowd cannot take it, they shove, lash out, trample those next to them to make a futile attempt to get through. British soldiers are stationed on either side of the street. They look distressed. No one has told them whether they should encourage people to stay or to go. Without any orders, they simply illustrate what the British Empire has become at the end of its mandate in Palestine: useless and helpless.

"Arabs of Haifa, do not leave!"

A loud, electrifying voice rings out above the thick motion-less crowd. They look all around them. They recognize the speaker's peculiar accent in Arabic: it is Shabatai Levy, the city's mayor.

"Return to your homes! Hang a white sheet from your balcony, no one will hurt you!"

Najjar sees the white car parked on a promontory, broadcasting the message through a bullhorn. The car is surrounded by armed Jews. Najjar doesn't know what to think. Appointed by the British, Shabatai Levy was relatively well accepted by the Palestinians because of his Arab origins. But why is he asking the residents to stay when the army of the Jews is shelling Haifa for the very purpose of getting them to leave? The car heads off, repeating its shouted message, giving rise to the same feeling of misunderstanding and mistrust.

"We can't trust the Jews!" one man suddenly shouts. "Remember Deir Yassin!"

That name alone is enough to electrify people: "Deir Yassin!" "The Jews are coming!" "Allahu akbar!" "Everyone to the port!" Miraculously, they are able to move forward. Even if he wanted to change his mind, Najjar no longer has that choice: the crowd is carrying him along yet again.

The sun is rising over the thousands of men, women and children massed along the waterfront and in the streets and on the surrounding beaches. The actual port has been occupied by the Haganah, who are allowing no one to enter. The immense crowd is seeking only a way to the sea, any way. Najjar is pushed forward, even though he is afraid of water and does not know how to swim. Prisoner of the multitude, he is pushed yard by yard closer to the launches, fishing boats, coasters, yachts, and barges, all of which are taken by storm by the fleeing populace. Shells continue to rain down from Mount Carmel, driving them ever faster. Holding their children in their arms, the men and women in the first rows try to board the boats. But the pressure is so great that many of them fall into the water. Hindered by their clothes, those who fear they will drown, because they are too young or too old or too weak, are shouting and struggling and reaching out in desperation. One enormous rowboat heavy with clusters of families pulls away from the shore, while soaked wraiths, dragging their suit-cases and their offspring, run behind it in the water. One of the fishermen on board slams his oar against the fingers of those clinging to the hull, but there are too many trying to climb on board. Thirty yards away, on the beach, Najjar watches as the giant boat heels and capsizes, spilling its human cargo into the sea. A single unanimous scream rises from the surface of the water. Other rowboats try to leave the shore, fights break out, everyone is looking only to save their own life, while people drown in the general indifference.

Several British launches eventually arrive on the scene. Through the bullhorn, His Majesty's sailors announce that those who so desire may come on board provided they do so in an orderly and disciplined fashion. In reply come volleys of insults and screams of rage. The launches are overwhelmed just as the other boats were. In vain the sailors fire into the sky, lash out with their rifle butts: there is no stopping the momen-tum. Those who got there first are able to clamber on board, further enraging the people left behind. Najjar manages to wedge himself against a wall and stands stock still. People are sliding along the waterfront as if it were a moving carpet; they fall into the water, whole clusters at a time. Those who don't drown lose all their belongings. All of them, however, dead or alive, are keeping, deep in their pocket and wrapped in a hand-kerchief, the key for their return.

To Go, to Stay - 1948

A lbert has no idea how long Najjar has been gone. He drops off to sleep and wakes up in the same place, as if he'd passed out, on the lawn in the garden. He's not really asleep, it's just that there are images which are so persistent that they stretch time and abolish it. Whatever he does, he remains restless. The human mass around the port seems immobile, an organic shape with shifting contours, a swarm of activity ringed by red and yellow explosions, like fireworks. This prickly feeling is in his own body, nothing is happening, his eyes burn with tears from staring so intently at the same place. The image blurs, becomes vague and then imprints itself upon his mind.

He lowers his gaze then looks up again. A long dazzling arm has emerged from the human magma: the road to Lebanon, the artery from which the blood is seeping, uncontrollably. He shakes his head to try to remain present. From this distance it is hard to believe that this unchanging river is made of people. Cars, carts, horses are stuck among them, their scarcely perceptible forward movement measures the rhythm of flight. He watches, cannot stop watching, it is all recorded, slowly, enduringly. His city is emptying out before his eyes, he himself is emptying out.

He wakes again. Perhaps he really has slept this time. How can he tell? Night is falling, darkness spreading over the city like a cloak. Darkness gradually winning, not a single light is lit. The electricity has not been cut, however. He cannot understand why his chest feels so unbearably tight. He knows, but does not want to know. Everyone has left. He is alone on his hill.

Projectors are lit, the port is ablaze with light, revealing a hubbub of activity. It's day and night, the frontier where a new story begins. Boats at anchor are unloaded by giant cranes while others wait their turn. Military vehicles, cannons, weapons, ammunition all pass over people's heads and are piled up on the dock. Soldiers running this way and that. They've won, they're in a hurry, they no longer need to hide. The trucks they have loaded up leave the port and weave their way through town. Their headlights trace lines of light in the darkness.

She says she has just arrived in Haifa, on a mission, the center of town has upset her terribly, visions, a nightmare, an enormous body emptied of life. She is three feet away from him, how did she get in? He is standing too, perhaps to greet her, he can't really recall. She came up to the Pink House as quickly as she could, she hasn't managed to fail to remember, she was afraid he too might have left. He looks at her, it isn't her, she isn't here. She's a ghost of herself.

Gently, she takes her lover's face in her hands and kisses him. He returns her kiss, timidly. Her lips are slightly salty. The port, perhaps, by the shore. What is she doing here? Perhaps she belongs to the delegation who have come to take possession of the ghost of the city, there is always such a delegation. She observes him in silence. She is looking at him with her entire face, her nose, her chin, her round chest. He recognizes her. Her eyes are sharp. She has come to ask him to stay. The Arabs of Haifa must stay, it's very important. What is she talking about? To go, to stay, he hasn't even been giving it any further thought. What does she want from him? She has nothing else to say. Her expression is exalted, awestruck, Haifa has just fallen. He wouldn't say that she is joyful, no, he knows what she looks like when she is joyful. He remembers. There, a shadow has crossed her face, he sees the shadow, clearly, dark, stubborn, deep. Her silence is immense, there are too many dead, her own people, too human. He cannot find a trace of himself in her silence.

He hesitates. Her face is half concealed by night. He has the impression he is open to all the points of the compass. Why is she standing? She is looking through him, he has become transparent. He is afraid, she is so real. She is still talking, he cannot concentrate anymore, but who is she talking to?

A Few Historical References

1917 The British Foreign Secretary, Lord James Balfour, informs the Zionist leaders that the British Empire views favorably the creation of a Jewish national homeland in Palestine. The declaration provokes anger among the Arabs.

1917-1921 The British army occupies the country. The Ottoman Empire collapses. The League of Nations entrusts Great Britain with a mandate over Palestine. Arabs riot against Jewish immigration and land purchase.

1929 Clashes in Jerusalem between Jews and Arabs over the Wailing Wall. The British are overwhelmed. Massacre in the Jewish community in Hebron. All Jews leave Hebron.

1930 The British Government publishes a White Paper advocating a halt to all Jewish immigration in Palestine, then changes its mind. Renewed Arab rioting.

1933 To escape the Nazis, German and Austrian Jews begin flooding into Palestine.

1936-1939 Arab uprising lasting three years, eventually crushed. The British publish a new White Paper suggesting the division of the country. The Arabs reject it.

1939-1945 World War. The British attempt to stabilize the situation in Palestine without real success. At the end of the war, the discovery of the reality of the Holocaust shocks the world.

1945-1947 The United States gradually replaces Great Britain as protectors of the nascent Jewish state of Israel. Great Britain prepares to end its mandate in Palestine.

1947-1948 The U.N. proposes a plan for a separation which the Jews accept and the Arabs reject. The British withdraw. The state of Israel is proclaimed on May 14, 1948. Some seven hundred thousand Palestinians take the road to exile. The Arab armies intervene. They are defeated and driven out.

My thanks to Fuad el-Khoury who told me his story, to Julien Haussen for diligently rereading the manuscript, to Judith Brouste for her openness, to Jean-Daniel Baltassat for his trust, to Bernard Barrault and Leonello Brandolini for their patience, and to my daughter Assia Nassib-Turquier-Zauberman, for always.

About the Author

Sélim Nassib was born in Beirut in 1946 and currently lives in Paris. Throughout the 1980s, during the war in Lebanon, he served as a correspondent for the French newspaper *Libération*. He is also well known for his articles appearing in other high-profile periodicals. In 1990, he ended his career as journalist and has since dedicated himself full-time to literature. In addition to *The Palestinian Lover*, he is the author of *I Loved You for Your Voice* (Europa Editions 2006).

About Europa Editions

"To insist that if work is good, no matter what, people will read it? Crazy! But perhaps that's why I like Europa . . . They believe in what they are doing above everything. Viva Europa Editions!"
—ALICE SEBOLD, author of *The Lovely Bones*

"A new and, on first evidence, excellent source for European fiction for English-speaking readers."—JANET MASLIN, *The New York Times*

"Europa Editions has its first indie bestseller, Elena Ferrante's *The Days of Abandonment*."—*Publishers Weekly*

"We certainly like what we've seen so far."—*The Complete Review*

"A distinctly different brand of literary pleasure, thoughtfulness and, yes, even entertainment."—*The Ruminator*

"You could consider Europa Editions, the sprightly new publishing venture [...] based in New York, as a kind of book club for Americans who thirst after exciting foreign fiction."—*LA Weekly*

"Europa Editions invites English-speaking readers to 'experience all the color, the exuberance, the violence, the sounds and smells of the Mediterranean,' with an intriguing selection of the crème de la crème of continental noir."—*Murder by the Bye*

"Readers with a taste—even a need—for an occasional inky cup of bitter honesty should lap up *The Goodbye Kiss* . . . the first book of Carlotto's to be published in the United States by the increasingly impressive new Europa Editions."—*Chicago Tribune*

www.europaeditions.com

AVAILABLE NOW FROM EUROPA EDITIONS

The Days of Abandonment
Elena Ferrante
Fiction - 192 pp - $14.95 - isbn 1-933372-00-1

"Stunning . . . The raging, torrential voice of the author is something rare."—*The New York Times*

"I could not put this novel down. Elena Ferrante will blow you away."
—ALICE SEBOLD, author of *The Lovely Bones*

Rarely have the foundations upon which our ideas of motherhood and womanhood rest been so candidly questioned. This compelling novel tells the story of one woman's headlong descent into what she calls an "absence of sense" after being abandoned by her husband. Olga's "days of abandonment" become a desperate, dangerous freefall into the darkest places of the soul as she roams the empty streets of a city that she has never learned to love. When she finds herself trapped inside the four walls of her apartment in the middle of a summer heat wave, Olga is forced to confront her ghosts, the potential loss of her own identity, and the possibility that life may never return to normal again.

www.europaeditions.com

Troubling Love
Elena Ferrante
Fiction - 144 pp - $14.95 - isbn 1-933372-16-8

"It's the first time a novel ever made me get physical, and it was the first good mood I'd been in for weeks."—*The New York Times*

"Like Joyce's *Ulysses*, this journey draws vigorously on its cityscape. Naples is one of those sun-drenched spooky cities, thrumming with life and populated by ghosts, spastic with impermeable local culture."—*Time Out New York*

Following her mother's untimely and mysterious death, Delia embarks on a voyage of discovery through the streets of her native Naples searching for the truth about her family. Reality is buried somewhere in the fertile soil of memory, and Delia is determined to find it. This stylish fiction from the author of The Days of Abandonment is set in a beguiling but often hostile Naples, whose chaotic, suffocating streets become one of the book's central motifs. A story about mothers and daughters, and the complicated knot of lies and emotions that binds them.

Cooking with Fernet Branca
James Hamilton-Paterson
Fiction - 288 pp - $14.95 - isbn 1-933372-01-X

"A work of comic genius."—*The Independent*

"Provokes the sort of indecorous involuntary laughter that has more in common with sneezing than chuckling. Imagine a British John Waters crossed with David Sedaris."—*The New York Times*

Gerald Samper, an effete English snob, has his own private hilltop in Tuscany where he wiles away his time working as a ghostwriter for celebrities and inventing wholly original culinary concoctions—including ice-cream made with garlic and the bitter, herb-based liqueur of the book's title. Gerald's idyll is shattered by the arrival of Marta, on the run from a crime-riddled former soviet republic. A series of hilarious misunderstands brings this odd couple into ever closer and more disastrous proximity.

www.europaeditions.com

Minotaur
Benjamin Tammuz
Fiction/Noir - 192 pp - $14.95 - isbn 1-933372-02-8

"A novel about the expectations and compromises that humans create for themselves . . . Very much in the manner of William Faulkner and Lawrence Durrell."—*The New York Times*

An Israeli secret agent falls hopelessly in love with a young English girl. Using his network of contacts and his professional expertise, he takes control of her life without ever revealing his identity. *Minotaur* is a complex and utterly original story about a solitary man driven from one side of Europe to the other by his obsession.

Total Chaos
Jean-Claude Izzo
Fiction/Noir - 256 pp - $14.95 - isbn 1-933372-04-4

"Rich, ambitious and passionate . . . his sad, loving portrait of his native city is amazing."—*The Washington Post*

"Full of fascinating characters, tersely brought to life in a prose style that is (thanks to Howard Curtis' shrewd translation) traditionally dark and completely original."—*The Chicago Tribune*

This first installment in the legendary *Marseilles Trilogy* sees Fabio Montale turning his back on a police force marred by corruption and racism and taking the fight against the mafia into his own hands.

Chourmo
Jean-Claude Izzo
Fiction/Noir - 256 pp - $14.95 - isbn 1-933372-17-6

"This hard-hitting series captures all the world-weariness of the contemporary European crime novel, but Izzo mixes it with a hero who is as virile as he is burned out."—*Booklist*

"Chourmo . . . the rowers in a galley. In Marseilles, you weren't just from one neighborhood, one project. You were chourmo. In the same galley, rowing! Trying to get out. Together." In this second installment of Izzo's legendary Marseilles Trilogy (*Total Chaos, Chourmo, Solea*) Fabio Montale has left a police force riddled with corruption, racism and greed to follow the ancient rhythms of his native town: the sea, fishing, the local bar, hotly-contested games of belote. But his cousin's son has gone missing and Montale is dragged back onto the mean streets of a violent, crime-infested Marseilles.

The Big Question
Wolf Erlbruch
Children's Illustrated Fiction - 52 pp - $14.95 - isbn 1-933372-03-6

Named Best Book at the 2004 Children's Book Fair in
Bologna.

"[*The Big Question*] offers more open-ended answers than the likes
of Shel Silverstein's *Giving Tree* (1964) and is certain to leave even
younger readers in a reflective mood."—*Kirkus Reviews*

A stunningly beautiful and poetic illustrated book for children that
poses the biggest of all big questions: why am I here? A chorus of
voices—including the cat's, the baker's, the pilot's and the soldier's—offers us some answers. But nothing is certain, except that
as we grow each one of us will pose the question differently and be
privy to different answers.

The Butterfly Workshop
Wolf Erlbruch
Children's Illustrated Fiction - 40 pp - $14.95 - isbn 1-933372-12-5

Illustrated by the winner of the 2006 Hans Christian Andersen Award.

For children and adults alike . . . Odair, one of the "Designers of All Things" and grandson of the esteemed inventor of the rainbow, has been banished to the insect laboratory as punishment for his overactive imagination. But he still dreams of one day creating a cross between a bird and a flower. Then, after a helpful chat with a dog . . .

The Goodbye Kiss
Massimo Carlotto
Fiction/Noir - 192 pp - $14.95 - isbn 1-933372-05-2

"The best living Italian crime writer."—*Il Manifesto*

"A nasty, explosive little tome warmly recommended to fans of James M. Cain for its casual amorality and truly astonishing speed."—*Kirkus Reviews*

An unscrupulous womanizer, as devoid of morals now as he once was full of idealistic fervor, returns to Italy where he is wanted for a series of crimes. To avoid prison he sells out his old friends, turns his back on his former ideals, and cuts deals with crooked cops. To earn himself the guise of respectability he is willing to go even further, maybe even as far as murder.

Death's Dark Abyss
Massimo Carlotto
Fiction/Noir - 192 pp - $14.95 - isbn 1-933372-18-4

"Beneath the conventions of Continental noir is a remarkable study of corruption and redemption in a world where revenge is best served ice-cold."—*Kirkus* (starred review)

"Dark and, in part, extremely brutal stuff, but an interesting game of taking action and responsibility, of being able to—and not being able to — forgive and make sacrifices."—*The Complete Review*

A riveting drama of guilt, revenge, and justice, Massimo Carlotto's *Death's Dark Abyss* tells the story of two men and the savage crime that binds them. During a robbery, Raffaello Beggiato takes a young woman and her child hostage and later murders them. Beggiato is arrested, tried, and sentenced to life. The victims' father and husband, Silvano, plunges into an ever-deepening abyss until the day, years later, when the murderer seeks his pardon and Silvano turns predator as he ruthlessly plots his revenge.

Hangover Square
Patrick Hamilton
Fiction/Noir - 280 pp - $14.95 - isbn 1-933372-06-0

"Hamilton is a sort of urban Thomas Hardy: always a pleasure to read, and as social historian he is unparalleled."—NICK HORNBY

Adrift in the grimy pubs of London at the outbreak of World War II, George Harvey Bone is hopelessly infatuated with Netta, a cold, contemptuous, small-time actress. George also suffers from occasional blackouts. During these moments one thing is horribly clear: he must murder Netta.

www.europaeditions.com

I Loved You for Your Voice
Sélim Nassib
Fiction - 256 pp - $14.95 - isbn 1-933372-07-9

"Om Kalthoum is great. She really is."—BOB DYLAN

"In rapt, lyrical prose, Paris-based writer and journalist Nassib spins a rhapsodic narrative out of the indissoluble connection between two creative souls inextricably bound by their art."— *Kirkus Reviews* (starred)

Love, desire, and song set against the colorful backdrop of modern Egypt. The story of the Arab world's greatest and most popular singer, Om Kalthoum, told through the eyes of the poet Ahmad Rami, who wrote her lyrics and loved her in vain all his life. Spanning over five decades in the history of modern Egypt, this passionate tale of love and longing provides a key to understanding the soul, the aspirations and the disappointments of the Arab world.

Love Burns
Edna Mazya
Fiction/Noir - 192 pp - $14.95 - isbn 1-933372-08-7

"This book, which has Woody Allen overtones, should be of great interest to readers of black humor and psychological thrillers."
—*Library Journal* (starred)

"Starts out as a psychological drama and becomes a strange, funny, unexpected hybrid: a farce thriller. A great book."—*Ma'ariv*

Ilan, a middle-aged professor of astrophysics, discovers that his young wife is having an affair. Terrified of losing her, he decides to confront her lover instead. Their meeting ends in the latter's murder—the unlikely murder weapon being Ilan's pipe—and in desperation, Ilan disposes of the body in the fresh grave of his kindergarten teacher. But when the body is discovered . . .

www.europaeditions.com

Departure Lounge
Chad Taylor
Fiction/Noir - 176 pp - $14.95 - isbn 1-933372-09-5

"Smart, original, surprising and just about as cool as a novel can get
. . . Taylor can flat out write."—*The Washington Post*

"Entropy noir . . . The hypnotic pull lies in the zigzag dance of its
forlorn characters, casting a murky, uneasy sense of doom."
—*The Guardian*

A young woman mysteriously disappears. The lives of those she has
left behind—family, acquaintances, and strangers intrigued by her
disappearance—intersect to form a captivating latticework of coin-
cidences and surprising twists of fate. Urban noir at its stylish and
intelligent best.

www.europaeditions.com

The Jasmine Isle
Ioanna Karystiani
Fiction - 176 pp - $14.95 - isbn 1-933372-10-9

"Grim yet gorgeous, here's a modern Greek tragedy about love foredoomed, family life as battlefield, the wisdom and wantonness of the human heart and the implacable finality of the hand of fate."—*Kirkus Reviews*

A modern love story with the force of an ancient Greek tragedy. Set on the spectacular Cycladic island of Andros, *The Jasmine Isle*, one of the finest literary achievements in contemporary Greek literature, recounts the story of the old sea wolf, Spyros Maltambès, and the beautiful Orsa Saltaferos, sentenced to marry a man she doesn't love and to watch while the man she does love is wed to another.

Boot Tracks
Matthew F. Jones
Fiction/Noir - 208 pp - $14.95 - isbn 1-933372-11-7

"Mr. Jones has created a powerful blend of love and violence, of the grotesque and the tender."
—*The New York Times*

"More than just a very good crime thriller, this dark but illuminating novel shows us the psychopathology of the criminal mind . . . A nightmare thriller with the power to haunt."
—*Kirkus Reviews* (starred)

Charlie Rankin has recently been released from prison, but prison has not released its grip on him. He owes his life to "The Buddha," who has given him a job to do on the outside: he must kill a man, a man who has done him no harm, a man he has never met. Along the road to this brutal encounter, Rankin meets Florence, who may be an angel in disguise or simply a lonely ex porn star seeking salvation. Together they careen towards their fate, taking the reader along for the ride. A commanding, stylishly written novel that tells the harrowing story of an assassination gone terribly wrong and the man and woman who are taking their last chance to find a safe place in a hostile world.

Dog Day
Alicia Giménez-Bartlett
Fiction/Noir - 208 pp - $14.95 - isbn 1-933372-14-1

"In Nicholas Caistor's smooth translation from the Spanish, Giménez-Bartlett evokes pity, horror and laughter with equal adeptness. No wonder she won the Femenino Lumen prize in 1997 as the best female writer in Spain."—*The Washington Post*

In this hardboiled fiction for dog lovers and lovers of dog mysteries, detective Petra Delicado and her maladroit sidekick, Garzon, investigate the murder of a tramp whose only friend is a mongrel dog named Freaky. One murder leads to another and Delicado finds herself involved in the sordid, dangerous world of fight dogs. *Dog Day* is first-rate entertainment.

Carte Blanche
Carlo Lucarelli
Fiction/Noir - 120 pp - $14.95 - isbn 1-933372-15-X

"This is Alan Furst country, to be sure."—*Booklist*

April 1945, Italy. Commissario De Luca is heading up a dangerous investigation into the private lives of the rich and powerful during the frantic final days of the fascist republic. The hierarchy has guaranteed De Luca their full cooperation, so long as he arrests the "right" suspect. The house of cards built by Mussolini in the last months of WWII is collapsing and De Luca faces a world mired in sadistic sex, dirty money, drugs and murder.

www.europaeditions.com

Old Filth
Jane Gardam
Fiction - 256 pp - $14.95 - isbn 1-933372-13-3

"Jane Gardam's beautiful, vivid and defiantly funny novel is a must."—*The Times*

"This remarkable novel . . . will bring immense pleasure to readers who treasure fiction that is intelligent, witty, sophisticated and—a quality encountered all too rarely in contemporary culture—adult."—*The Washington Post*

Sir Edward Feathers has progressed from struggling young barrister to wealthy expatriate lawyer to distinguished retired judge, living out his last days in comfortable seclusion in Dorset. The engrossing and moving account of his life, from birth in colonial Malaya, to Wales, where he is sent as a "Raj orphan," to Oxford, his career and marriage, parallels much of the 20th century's dramatic history.